"The Final Curtain a Love Story Untold"

❦

"friendfromyesteryear"

ISBN: 150069651X
ISBN 13: 9781500696511
Library of Congress Control Number: 2014913753
CreateSpace Independent Publishing Platform
North Charleston, South Carolina

An Open Letter
To All The Fans of ...
"Elvis Aaron Presley"
(and those who wish they were!)

"Mystrykitty"

Well, we finally made it!
"The Final Curtain a Love Story Untold"
...until now,
has been completed, and
"Published."
Let me begin by saying the following:
In no way will this "Book" bring any "Disrespect"
to the "Presley" family, nor will it "Say Anything"
to "Tarnish" the image of a man who "gave
it all," right to the end, Our "friend"
"Elvis Aaron Presley,"

"The King of Rock & Roll."

◁───♡

"I"... "friendfromyesteryear," & "Mystrykitty" (my trusty companion, consultant, and "little pal"), wish to Thank You All for your thoughtful comments and fine expressions of "LOVE" on our "Channel." You have shown Outstanding "Respect" for The "Memory" of Our "friend"

"Elvis Aaron Presley."

"I," also am A "friend" as some of you already know, who lived back in those "Early" days of Rock & Roll. The days of "Yesteryear." "It was a "Different World" in those days. I was a young man and of course a "Fan" of Elvis. Who in their right mind wasn't back in those 1950's? (although there were some.)

The 1950's were "Remembered" by many as

"The Fabulous Fifties." for those of us growing up during that decade a "Change" in the music world was about to manifest itself. Yes "Change" was coming, and "What a Change!" Not a gentle "Evolution" OH NO! It would be an "EARTHQUAKE" of "Historical" proportions. Yes it would "Shake" the entire World!

That "Earthquake" came from a young "dirt poor boy" then living in "Memphis TN. U.S.A.

His Name....."Elvis Aron Presley."*

What this young man would accomplish in some 21 years would "Stagger" the Entertainment business, although Elvis Passed away on August 16,1977, His Music, Movies, Incredible Voice, Love for his fellow man, and incredible "Generosity" continue to be "Legendary."

And so His "Story" continues to be told from one generation to another.

"Elvis Aaron Presley" was and still remains a "Legend."

Annually "fans" gather from all over the world in "Memphis Tennessee" to memorialize his death at "Graceland" on 8/15-16, and return in December for Christmas at "Graceland" the "Home" of Elvis Presley. In January on the 8th day of the month they arrive again to celebrate his birth. And this has been going on for 35+ years. What attracts all these people from all ethnic, religious and many Nations annually ?

"LOVE"

This man, Elvis Presley, was and "still is loved" by "Millions."

Yes That "RUMBLE" continues to "Echo" right down into our day. He was a "Humble man" and a "friend" to millions. As He once stated, He believed He was living a "fairytale" life. "WE" all know "fairytales" all end happily.

The "Fictionalized" Story, "The Final Curtain a Love Story Untold" until now..will bring to light "Proof" that "fairytales" still have happy endings.....although the "Ending" isn't always what we might expect.

I, am "friend"......from......yesteryear

"The Final Curtain a Love Story Untold" **until now, is a "Fictional Story" about 4 individuals each from dif-ferent backgrounds. Three of these "individuals join together in "Search" for the "Ultimate Answer."**

Did Elvis Presley really Pass Away on August 16, 1977...Or did He "fake" His death and if so then WHY?

The fourth individual is a *"Surprise Searcher"* who will provide much in the way of relevant "Information." *Keep on the "Lookout" for the fourth "Searcher"* He will "cause you to ask many questions, but He will also *Provide needed*

"LIGHT" which will allow us to "SEE" a little at a time, what we may be *"allowed to know,"* but be very careful because the "Light" if abused can be "BLINDING."

What each "Searcher" finds is not what they "Expect to find," but be assured My "Readers" Each "receives" What Each Deserves!

By means of a "Fictional" account you will find "answers" including "The Ultimate Answer," but can you believe them?.........after all.....this is.....a...... "fictional Account." *Can any "Truth" be found in "fiction?".....Guard your "HEART" use your "HEAD" you are in for one amazing Ride!*

May "The Final Curtain a Love Story Untold"... until now bring "Peace & Happiness" and a sense of "Closure," to all who have shared a "Common Bond in Life," Their "Love & Respect for ....the "poor boy" from Tupelo...our "friend" Elvis Aaron Presley.....

May the story of "HIS" life "Continue to be Told" for he indeed taught us much about Love, Life, & "Sharing."

I consider this to be my final "Opus," it is my "gift," from my "heart" and I give it

TO "YOU"...my "friends"

"friendfromyesteryear"

Now possibly You may be wondering,

1. *"friendfromyesteryear" "Why did you write this "Fictional Book?" (This will be answered in this "fictional account.")*
2. *"Is it possible to find any "Truth" in "Fiction?"..(?)*
3. *"What will "The Final Curtain a Love Story Untold?" have to "say?".....(MUCH)*
4. *"Will it "silence" those who would "ridicule" Elvis ?(The rude, crass, ignorant, and "Trouble" makers will be here until this "old world" is gone.)*

5. *What will it have to say about 8/16/77?" (...Be alert, what do you think my dear "friends?")*
6. *"Will we learn anything "New" about Elvis?" (Always)*
7. *Will I "find" what "I've" been looking for? (That will be based on "WHAT" you are looking for.)*

If your questions... COME from your "HEART," you WILL "Understand, and Receive your "Answers," and why is this the case? Simply because "The Final Curtain" is

*"Truly" a "LOVE STORY" of **"Enormous proportion."***

(But of course that will have to be "your" decision after you have read the "Book" the FIRST time, I've read it more times than I can count)

∽

- *As "Our Journey" begins you will quickly understand where we are headed, hang in there to the "End," the "read" is lenghty in places. Don't look ahead as it will ruin the "emotional impact" of "The Story," and even worse YOU WILL BE SO CONFUSED YOU WON'T KNOW "UP" from "DOWN."*
- *Be careful, read slowly, you may have to read this account twice or else you'll find yourself so far in the woods even "Daniel Boone," an "American Frontiersman," wouldn't be able to find you! Use your "Compass" your "HEAD" to guide you on your journey. Be careful you're not misled, why? Because if we let our "Hearts" lead us we could be headed for "trouble." Why again? As Elvis once told the small "Bible" group he was conversing with, before they began to sing some "Gospel," "The Heart is more "Treacherous" than anything else and WHO can know it?" (Jeremiah 19:9) Therefore we need to be careful that we don't let our "Hearts" overrule our clear thinking faculties. In our "Journey," we will find ourselves "Traveling" with "Characters" who carry along with "THEM Serious excess "Baggage," the full range of human emotion and curosity. "Mystery", "Search", "Discovery", "Greed", "Reward", "Loyalty" "True Friendship", and sadly "Deceit." So be Careful &... "Stay alert!"*

Always *"Remember," In no way will I, "friendfromyesteryear," allow this "Book" to bring any "Disrespect" to the "Presley" family, nor will it say anything to "Tarnish" the image of a man who "gave it all," right to the end. Our "friend" Elvis "Aaron" Presley. Indeed, "The King of Rock & Roll."*

Now before we begin "Our Journey," I would like to take just a couple of minutes to thank all the "Fans of Elvis" who have been very supportive of my "Youtube Channel," encouraging me and "mystrykitty" (my little pal), also helping with research to make the channel's comments interesting & accurate. And because of your help, "I"... "friendfromyesteryear" & "Mystrykitty" (my trusty companion, consultant, and "little pal"), have been seen pretty much "Worldwide"

- ***"Special thanks"*** *to, (here's where I get myself in trouble when I "FORGET" someone's name. I'll have to invoke my right to say at my age my mind does at times get a little "fuzzy."..LOL) You fans of "Elvis," have made the channel "what it is." I sincerely thank you "ALL"*

- *...Remember I could not list all the fine comments, or else you would never get to read the book! maybe I'll publish a book containing nothing but comments from his fans. we'll have too see what the future holds and what you dear friends would like. .....So I chose **"Seven"** "friends" with "differing backgrounds" but all are "Fans of Elvis." Please don't feel left out...for you're all in my "Heart."* ***And so "Special Thanks" to the following people:***

- *Miss Lisa A. (It's been a real "Joy" meeting such a nice young lady from "France"...Miss Lisa send a big "Hello" to "Paris" for me and thank you for the "French Lessons... "merci" you've been a joy to know.), "je te souhaite une belle journée, mon ami" & God Bless... "friend")*

- *Miss doddie B. (you are The "Elvis" prize fighter.... "cut me I bleed.") Thanks for your encouraging comments and "loyalty"...you're one I certainly would want on my side! God Bless... "friend")*

- *Miss Mary M. (nice scarf you're wearing Mary! Was it a "Gift?" From Who? LOL. We know "WHO" and so it's a "Treasure." Thanks for your loving comments...another nice young Lady... God Bless "friend").*

- *Miss joyce G. (Thank you for all your "enthusiam" and fine comments. So from one "Tennesseean" to another..God Bless ... "friend")*
- *Steve P. (...you Steve, have a very "Poetic" way of expressing yourself...very nice comments...God..... Bless... "friend"...)*
- *"Rodster" (You are a very "funny character" with some very "straight Forward but "insightful" comments...Thank you so much. You add a good sense of "Humor" to our Channel....God Bless.....friend")*
- *Stephen E. (you have been a very helpful "friend" with very good insight, and much knowledge about "Elvis." Thank you for being the "friend" you are... God Bless... "friend")*

*And of course I give a **"Great Big Thank You"** to my wife... **"Jean"**...She too is a "Fan of Elvis." (...of course!)*

She has had to put up with me for almost 50 years now....She's a real "Sweety pie." This "Book" has indeed taken me away from her for long periods of time, and I thank her for cooperating with me so that this "Timely" publication would be "Published" when the "Proper Time" had arrived.

So a "Big Thank You"
"Jean"...
for all your help and "Patience"...you have put up with "much."
"I love You."
And Now...
Some comments made by those listed in the "Thank You section."

Miss Lisa A.
1. To: friendfromyesteryear...
Bravo! My friend! You are on the right way, It's never too late. As we have not the same time. I was in my bed when you said Bonsoir, so I couldn't answer you directly. Now you are still sleeping and in France it's morning...c'est la vie: that's life! Now I'm saying: Bonjour to you. Je te souhaite une belle journée: I wish you a beautiful day!`

****

Miss doddie B.
2. To: friendfromyesteryear

Yes it is very beautiful...Friend, I read that the reason he was so stressed in Vegas when he was doing 2 shows a night, was because he wanted the second show to be as good as the first...He said it was a whole new audience and he wanted them to have the best too...Bless his heart, those years were hard...I wish they had invested for his future and he could have taken off and only worked when he wanted too...There was poor management for him....

Miss Mary M.
3. To: friendfromyesteryear

I have loved Elvis for years, since he first started. This concert just breaks my heart because I love him so. I firmly believe he was so tired and his manager pushed him too hard. I don't care what anyone says, he will ALWAYS be in my heart until I'm no longer on this earth. I was fortunate to see him in person 7 times in my life and I am so grateful that I will always love him.

Miss joyce G.
4a. To: friendfromyesteryear

I know you said the book was "fiction," but is it about Elvis's whole life. Maybe it won't be like the other books. I hope it tells it all and it's the real truth, no lies or parts added. Can't wait for it to come out!!! Thanks friend. (Thank You for your "Enthusiasm" Miss joyce)... "friend"

Steve P.

"The Final Curtain..." (1st video released concerning "Book" release). Stephen now describes very "poetically" the video he has just viewed on youtube.

5. To: friendfromyesteryear "Looking back on golden years at happy times, memories that came floating down all around, that seemed like it would last forever, until came a time of utter despair the realization that he was no longer there. We remember now the simple faith he had, that he often sang about and lived by which he always loved to share. Something that he hoped those that love him, family, friends and fans might accept as well so they can follow to meet their Lord, too when the final curtain comes down."

(beautifulandwellsaid, thankyouSteve..GodBless... "friendfromyesteryear")

6. ***"Rodster 300"***...*Why was I born 10 years after he retired...*
WHY!!! lol (you Rodster300 "R" "too funny!" LOL) ...God Bless...
"friendfromyesteryear

Stephen E. to ... "friendfromyesteryear"

Hi there friend...
I want to thank you ..
You have a true heart for Elvis.
Some think many things.
All was not as it appeared to be.
Elvis I am sure would be happy with your assessments. Although no-one can speak for him.
I like you & I know you are not using Elvis for money. The Corporations are those that I meant. There are some folks that hate Elvis due to the fact of jealousy that they don't receive the same attention as Elvis does.
No one can be another.
All folks must just be themselves.
Elvis is Elvis..
There is room for all in music as Elvis once said.
They just have to walk a mile in his shoes first.
Just what did Elvis gain or more to the point...what did he lose.
As I see it he gained the respect of his fans & then their love.
Their respect & love was all Elvis cared about or really ever wanted.

Your book....
I am sure will turn up the lights on high. And yes...life's lessons can help to see. Elvis in mind lived a full life of age & wisdom. And with your wisdom combined & things you know will make for an excellent book.
I think it is fine to also enjoy something from your very kind book. Elvis would see something like your book as fresh air If he could know.
I know you understand...
I know you will do his name a great respect & honor.
I think you would be a wonderful person to know.!!!
Thank you so much....Keep well & safe our friend.
Stephen E.

To Stephen...

You're a "True"... "friend"...Stephen, and thank you for your kind words...Maybe this book will get people's attention and help them to recognize the "Real from the Make Believe." Elvis made it very easy for us we just need to "Know Him"...Really "Know Him."...Good night or morning where ever you are...God Bless... "friendfromyesteryear"

                                ⤳

These were some of the 1,000's of comments made on my channel...

You fans of Elvis have made "Mystrykitty's Oldies" channel "what it is."

I sincerely Thank "You All!"

May The Final Curtain a "LOVE STORY" Untold, bring you "Peace in your "hearts"... for you Dear "fans" of "Elvis Aaron Presley" have suffered and grieved for a "very long time"....
this is my "Gift to You"...it comes from my "Heart"...

It's TIME!
"Welcome!"
To...
"The Final Curtain"
a "Love Story"
"Untold"...
Until now !
"friendfromyesteryear"

                                ⤳

"mystrykitty"

Chapter 1

The... "End or the Beginning?"

⌁

(NOW DON'T YOU PEEK AT THE LAST CHAPTER, *it will do you no good...you* NEED *the "Italic" points along the way to* "UNDERSTAND" *the full picture...(I love my "Elvis".. "Mystrykitty")* FOR "THEY" WILL HELP YOU TO UNDERSTAND WHAT WE Need" TO KNOW" *(those points are printed in type like you now see)....("Italic Print")*

⌁

"*August 16, 1977*"...Memphis Tennessee... A phone call has just come from Joe Esposito stating Elvis Presley has died. The news travels at Lightning speed throughout the entire world... Yes, The world is shocked! Could it be true, the "King of Rock & Roll" has really died?

As history would show, the "Final Curtain" had indeed come down on Elvis. He was truly "gone."

What would now unfold, in the next 72 hours, would bring many questions...questions that would take decades to find satisfying answers to. Yes the time

1

would eventually come to "Uncover" that which "some believe" may have been "Covered Over"

I AM ......"friendfromyesteryear" Welcome...to..... "The Final Curtain...a Love Story Untold" ...Until now.

Yes The "King of Rock & Roll," Elvis Presley, was indeed dead... or so believed.

Now THE fans begin to question, did He really die, or had he decided to "pack it in?" That would be the question that would take decades to answer and even then, could One be sure? It seemed the fans did not want to believe Elvis had truly "passed away." Many still believe today, He is alive and living "somewhere?"

What is the "Truth?" Most importantly is it "Possible" to really know for certain?

And even more importantly "Do we have the

"Right to Know?"...

Yes an "eye opening experience" awaits, as the "The "Final Curtain" is slowly "raised" to reveal One Lonely "Candle" burning in a darkened room.

Did Elvis pass away on 8/16/77 as we have been "told", or did "He orchestrate his demise." If so, is HE still with us?

On our Journey we will learn of 3 individuals who spent half their lives, in search for the "Truth" as to whether Elvis really died in "77"...what they eventually find, proves to be a "Lesson & Moral

for us all! As the "Curtain" begins to "rise," that one small "candle" burning in a darkened room will allow "ENOUGH" light for us to see much. But as we will find out in our story, too much "LIGHT" can be "Blinding!"

We now begin to see a man Betrayed, Deceived, and Lied to by so called "friends" from within his "inner circle."

A young man whose marriage had failed and the loves of his life, His daughter and wife, were now gone...

A child who would find it difficult growing up without her "daddy."

We will come to "know" a man with a deep "Spiritual Yearning" longing to have it filled.

Yes here He was, a man of enormous talent,

Loved by his fans, and yet his "Name," would make him a "prisoner, of his "fame."

How could this Tormented, aging, lonely, sad, and failing in health man, ever reach his hoped for goal...."TRUE SPIRITUAL FULFILLMENT,"

With a "family of friends" whom He could share & associate with on an intimate basis without being constantly bombarded by the "World" for "more", "more" and yet "more"...

He had lost his freedom, nowhere to 'run,' nowhere to 'hide.' At times He would have to use "Doubles" to 'escape' from Graceland, He indeed was a "Prisoner" of his fame. But that was not the end of it. Sadly he was also the object of "Death Threats." He had to act and act fast...the "clock" was ticking. He was now 42 years old, his health was in jeopardy, and there were some problems with his last "ConcertTour" in 1977. Most of the "77" concerts he did are no longer available for viewing. Some today believe there were 'powers' that felt Elvis should only be remembered as a "Young Man" who never

'Aged' beyond 33 years. He was living a "Fairytale Life" and it was time for the "Fairytale" to come to an "End".

On his "FINAL CURTAIN TOUR" Elvis sang 'fairytale', stating:

"This is the story of my life."

Was it time to make a 'decision', or had the "Decision" already been made... perhaps the "Die" was already "Cast," And NOT by Him. Indeed this would be a major dilemma for anyone, but for Elvis, if He were truly going to "fake" His death, with his money... his connections with "High Level" government officials, and "Extraordinary determination," it could be done.

He had indeed come to "The End of His Road." He had to make his exit. But would his exit be "Intentional, or Unintentional," that would be your job, Dear Reader to decide.

If He succeeded and did not really die. What would be the consequences? Would He just be exchanging one dilemma for another, and would living in exile be tantamount to "Imprisonment?"

It was indeed "Time" for Elvis to "TCB" And in a "Flash"... "HE" was "Gone!"

⟋⟍

Let us now pause
for a moment and reflect...

If Elvis truly died, then what would motivate people to search for what "They" would hope to find, so called proof of His "Great Escape?"

Would it be Curiosity, or a desire to capitalize on the knowledge, or write a book? (Money).

Or to cause him harm, or

*"I want to find him alive and living a happy life"...
(motive for search.)*

Yes there are many reasons why people are obsessed with Elvis Presley's "Death."

1. Some for "good" reasons. 2. Some for "selfish" reasons. 3. Some for "evil" reasons.

It is for "the reasons stated" that "Understanding" one's "Motive" for "Search," would help to distinguish between Those who are merely "Curious," curious not only out of "Love" for Elvis, but "hoping" He did survive, and that He was able to enjoy a life of peace & happiness

and

Then there are those who search for selfish reasons.

In almost ALL these cases the "motive" has to do with "Money."

So we need to be "serious" about this journey, with the "right motive" for the search and we must be "willing" to except "The Truth" as "real evidence" only would "Dictate."

To do otherwise would be only fooling ourselves...

The answers we receive to some of our biggest questions in life aren't always the answers we want to hear.

On the other hand one must not let emotion overrule clear thinking, or be deceived by those whom would "Tickle our ears" with what we would "like" to hear.

It is for "the reasons stated" that I will now tell you "My Story," A "Fictional" account concerning "August 16-18 "1977", & some years leading up to and after the tragic event on 8/16/77.

Recalling these events will bring "My Story" to an "End" And my "purpose" for being here at this time in "History" will also come to an "END."

You "WILL" understand "WHY," as we move along in our story.

So now I ask you,

"Dear Reader."

Is it "possible" to find any "Truth"

In "Fiction?"

That will be a question only "You" will decide after reading "My Story" at least twice.

Pay close attention as we "Journey together" down this "bumpy road" of some 10 years. The Story is unbelievable....

* But then, it's only... "Fiction."...

Let "Common Sense Rule" in your judgement and I promise you, when all is said and done you will rejoice at what your search will "Truly Reveal!" And so as we begin our "Journey," As miss "Lisa" a "friend" of mine from "France" might say ... "Bon Voyage"... and from me... "God Bless" & may "The Final Curtain...a Love Story Untold" bring you True Satisfaction, Peace of Mind & Joy of "Heart" for all the grief "ya'll" have suffered all these years... and

Wondering, "Did He make it?"

Chapter 2

The rush to rest...

∼◦

*I*t is now August 16th 1977. The world has been informed of the passing of "The King." We now find ourselves at "Graceland."

We seem to hear what appears to be
much commotion.... Join us as we "listen in" to the Conversation, it's a bit 'muffled' but lets try anyhow.

"So what's next?"...
A familiar voice now replies,
"Well..." he pauses...he appears extremely nervous, his face pales with anxiety and as he replies his voice begins to crack... tears are falling from his eyes,
"all" is being taken care of.
We all know what our responsibilities are at this point."
Another familiar voice interjects:
"What about all the contacts? Are you sure they've been notified?"

Obviously in great 'pain' he then asks:

*"And what are we to say to all the Fan clubs
that are already ringing the phones off the Hook.....
Oh God!!.... What will we say?"*

*"I've taken care of that and my instructions are that
all major Fan Clubs are to be contacted & those instructions are being carried out at this very moment."*

*"What are they being told to do, after all they'll be
clamoring to be here out of respect for Him."*

*"Zion get me my clipboard from my desk please. Let
me quote from my notes.*

*Our Intimate "Public Relations" people, will be
informed to communicate to all Fan Clubs on our
'Special Registry.' They are to be told to try and understand why we cannot accommodate their wishes and
delay this process. There is utter chaos here. Memphis
is overrun with grief. People are passing out all over
the place, some have gone into shock, and others have
been
Hospitalized and there is even greater sadness in that
we've received word ************(muffled Conversation)
and now there have been at least 2 fatalities due to
individuals being hit by vehicles... Men we want to
get this over as fast as possible or else we can expect
********* (Muffled Conversation) and if we extend the
Time period for the fan clubs, Memphis will
be overrun by hundreds of thousands, and the city
could not handle that large of a crowd. Neither could
the Hospital. I'm sure they will understand." All the
"other" contacts *************(muffled conversation)
made ***(muffled
conversation).*

Now the room takes on an even more solemn atmosphere. Some are just sitting, their hands clasped over their face.... They're crying....

They can't believe that Elvis is "gone"....There is "More Conversation" going on, but it is very difficult to hear at this time"... *********************careful.*

Has the "Final Curtain"
really come down on "The King?"
Or has something big, really "BIG" been perpetrated?
Are we looking at the "Story of The 20ᵗʰ Century," the "alleged" death of Elvis Aaron Presley...a 'cover-up?' and if a "Cover Up"... WHY?
It is now August 17ᵗʰ and the autopsy reports are in, the "Death Certificate" has been Signed, confirming the death of Elvis, and 17 White Cadillac's have been 'gathered' from all over the country for the "Funeral Procession."
There would be questions about the coroners Report and the "Death" certificate plus many other questions. As we continue down this "narrow & cramped road" the answers to many of these questions plus many others will become apparent. So please pay "close attention" as we "View" the "Funeral Procession," and subsequent events that occur "Rapidly," but first we must listen as best we can to what is happening back at Graceland. The 'conversation continues'. Let's listen in...

"Zion" have the "people" gotten in touch with you?No sir. But I did call them just moments ago."

"Fine job Zion!" Keep those boys busy.

We want all things to go smoothly.
There can be no .... ********************************
************************************** ********************
***(more   muffled*
conversation)...
We will also take care of "Security."
The "Memphis" police are at this VERY MOMENT on
alert and active. They have been a Great Help.
Try not to say************ ********************************
********************************** *"ok?".... (More muffled*
conversation)...
We now temporarily leave Memphis.
We will return shortly, but for now, we move on to
"View" what is happening "all around" us,
both "presently" and in recent "Years,"
leading up to the events that are unfolding
before
our very eyes today, August 16, 1977.

The events we will discuss would have a "Dramatic"
effect on Elvis, and the "Direction" His life would even-
tually take... leading to what has tragically occurred
today. (8/16/77)

Chapter 3

1963-68... "Marked years..."

Elvis "68" Comeback Special

❧

"*1 963*" would be a "marked year" for the U.S. It was November 22, 1963.

President John F. Kennedy was in Dallas Texas.

The weather was beautiful. He now, around noon-time, proceeded in His presidential limousine and motorcade down into town.

As they passed The "Texas Book Depository," turning down onto Houston Street, the crowds were lining the route of the Motorcade.

As the Motorcade passed, the people were smiling and applauding. The president's wife, Jacquelyn, said to the President:

"Well they certainly like you down here in Texas."
The President then said to his wife:

"They certainly do."

*Seconds later The President would be "Dead",
as an assassin's bullet would end His life.*

⤳

*Let us now speed up to 1968, five years after the assi-
nation of President John F. Kenneddy.*

*"1968" would be "Remembered" as the year the
Country changed dramatically.*

*The Vietnam War was intensifying, the country was
"Racially" divided and then on April 4th 1968 "Tragedy"
struck again...*

*Dr. Martin Luther King, while staying at the African
American owned Lorraine motel in Memphis Tennessee,
was assassinated by a single shot from a scope sighted
30.06 caliber Remington pump rifle, at a distance of
some 205 feet.*

*The shot entered Dr. King's neck severing his spinal
cord. Within one hour he was declared dead. His death
was the 12th Major death in the "civil rights" movement
since 1963.*

*On June 5th 1968, while running for his party's endorse-
ment for president of The United States, Senator Robert
Kennedy was "Downed" by an assassin with 3 shots.*

*One shot passing into his skull, shattering, frag-
menting, and mortally wounding the Senator. He later
died approximately 25 hours later.*

*The assassination of 2 major leaders within a period
of 9 weeks convinced many that the country was in a
downward "spiral," now "out of control."*

*It was at "This Time," in "American History," that
"ELVIS" decided to make his "Comeback."............*

*Meanwhile in the music world, the "British Invasion"
was in full swing. The 'Beatles,' The 'Rolling Stones'*

and many other British groups had 'Invaded' the Music World and taken "center stage."

1968 Would be a "happy time" for Elvis, he's happily married and has finished up His Movie contracts. He and His wife have just had the "Blessing" of the Birth of their 1st, and sadly to be only child. Yes a "Beautiful" baby girl. Her name is "Lisa Marie.

It has been about 7 years since Elvis performed before a live audience. We now listen to a conversation that's going on "backstage" at the "68" "Comeback Special," just prior to his going on stage.......
"Where's Elvis? He's supposed to go "on" in 10 minutes. Has anyone checked his dressing room? Carlo you're supposed to be with him until He goes on stage. WHERE IS HE!" Carlo replies nervously "I'll check His Dressing room." When Carlo gets there, what does he see?.....Elvis slumped over with his hands covering over His face. He approaches Him.. "Elvis, are you alright?" The 'silence' is deafening... "I can't do it.... It's been too long...(He now sighs), they've probably forgotten about me." "Don't be ridiculous, you're "The King"..Elvis.... YOU CAN DO IT!!" He's naturally very nervous about this "comeback." Will he be accepted by his fans or have they lost interest in him? Elvis stands up, Carlo embraces Him, it seems to Carlo like an eternity, Elvis now backs away and simply says.... "I'll do it..."
Elvis now appears before a small audience & with a small instrumental group. This performance becomes known as "The "68" Comeback Special." Elvis has missed the 'live' audiences but it IS a 'different time.' The music world has changed, would He still be excepted?......Time would tell!

A lean, clean, and absolutely good-looking man stands before us. He's dressed in what appears to be Black Leather...he is well tanned and a bit nervous. His Fans look "Admiringly" at Him as he performs again & again. They are absolutely "thrilled" at his performance. This "68" Comeback Special" goes down as a great success. The "KING" is Back and obviously his fans "NEVER FORGOT HIM," for they were thrilled beyond belief!

Yes the 'British Invasion' had changed the "scene" of the music world and if you were there, you would agree, Rock & Roll, as in the beginning, was never to be the same again, but "Elvis Presley" would NEVER ever again, be 'challenged,'.... as The "King" of Rock & Roll. (at least that would be true in my lifetime..... friendfromyesteryear).

Interestingly, as History would recall, After the "assassination" of Dr. Martin Luther King, Elvis' life would take on a "New Direction." He was known to say by his inner circle that He would "never" again allow himself to be forced to sing a song He didn't like. I guess that was a "message" to "Parker," his manager.

He then performed what many believe was one of His Greatest performances, in the "68" Comeback Special, "If I Can Dream." This was written for Elvis only weeks after the death of "Dr. Martin Luther King" The amazing similarities that seem to parallel Dr. Martin Luther King's famous "I Have A Dream" speech" are quite obvious in the words to "If I Can Dream" sung by ELVIS. Take time now, if you choose, to "Listen" to Elvis sing "If I Can Dream" It will help set the stage for what's "ahead."

As history would recall, the "68" Comeback Special" would be the 'Beginning' of a 'New' Elvis. His looks, persona, *Raw Talent*, would rip at the 'Hearts' of his fans...they would want more, more, and still more from their "King." Elvis would not disappoint His fans...yes HE would 'Give them something to "REMEMBER" & as History would record... "THEY NEVER FORGOT!"*

Chapter 4

Elvis...the "Spiritual" man...

⤜⤏

Yes, the "68" concert was indeed a tremendous success, but now we begin to see another side of Elvis...His "Spiritual" side, which would now play a big role in his life.

Join us as we "listen" into a conversation going on among some of his closest friends. They had just finished doing some Gospel songs. Elvis has just left the group to go upstairs.

He'll be just a few minutes. While He is gone "they are given strict orders" "NO MORE GOSPEL!"...Let's listen in and "see" what transpires.

"Now what will we do? I just don't know what to say to 'Him' when He comes down those stairs and tells us He wants to do another 'Gospel Song.' After all we've been warned, "No more 'Gospel'... that's NOT what I am paying Him to do."

"So when He gets here remember, all I want to hear is The Elvis I know...NO GOSPEL!"...

"Carlo, you're his best friend, you break it

to Him, gently...o.k.?"

"Forget about it! I'm not saying anything... you understand!"

"But"

"Never mind the buts...just keep it quiet and lets see what He does."

Elvis now starts down the stairs, everybody is nervous. He approaches the piano and states...

"Hey guys, how about another Gospel!"

Carlo timidly speaks up, "uh, uh, Elvis...we were told by, you know who, to make sure when you come down to this here piano, you go right to 'work' and you're to start singing some of those songs on that new album that you're being paid to make..."

"What!"

*Listen, if I want to sing Gospel I will
sing Gospel and you boys will
accompany me! ... And NO ONE is
gonna stop us...you got it?
O.K... then let's do it!"*

And so that night guess what, my dear reader, they sang Gospel and NO ONE, outside the 'group,' said boo! There were many other nights when they would sing Gospel, it was Elvis way, in His mind and heart, to Draw close to The "LORD."

*These Gospel sessions would raise
His spirit and obviously the spirit of those
who sang with Him. In time it would become
a practice to include at least one Gospel song
in every Concert.
At one particular concert a group of girls
purchased tickets for an entire row. They were
about 8 or 10 rows back from the front
of the stage where Elvis was performing. When He*

finished his performance, the girls
immediately stood up. In their hands was a 'scroll'
that they unrolled. It filled the entire row of seats.
Quickley they raised it.
It read "Elvis is The King!" They
then chanted "Elvis is the King"...with that Elvis
stopped
the show, quieted the people, and while pointing
to those girls
at the top of his lungs said,
"I'M Not The King, JESUS CHRIST is THE KING!
Now roll that thing up and sit down!"

Well let me tell you, those girls put down their banner, sat down and didn't say a word! They knew He meant it!

Yes although Elvis was loved by millions, He knew His rightful place, He was not a "God" to be worshipped, neither a "King" to be adored...yes as Elvis would say, "I'm not a King, I'm just a man"...Yes, He indeed was a man, and a "Humble" one at that!

Certainly there are many stories one
could write about Elvis. Stories of how he would give tremendous gifts away, automobiles, watches,
jewelry, vacations etc.
His great love for "Almighty God," and HIS dear son, Jesus....

His love for the Word of God, The "BIBLE" and on numerous occasions, quoting from it.
About 2 years before His "death," Rex Humbard, a member of the clergy was in Las Vegas, and was hoping to get some tickets for
The "ElvisVegas Concert."

His people contacted Elvis' people to see what they could do to get tickets. Now Rex was a close friend of the Presley family and had "officiated" at the Memorial

Services of Gladys Presley when she had passed.

They gave the phone to Elvis & Elvis told him,

"Don't worry they'll be seats for you and your party, and after the show I'll take you backstage."

Well Rex Humbard showed up that night,

with his party, and indeed they all had a wonderful time.

Interestingly that night would not become

a night neither Elvis, nor Rex, would ever forget.

Let's listen in to what transpired that night after the show.

"Elvis thank you so much for the tickets, they told us the concert was all sold out when we tried to buy tickets."

"That's true sir, but we keep a few for special guests and you sir are a very special guest."

"Well thank you so much Elvis. I enjoyed the concert and so did my friends."

"Well thank you again Sir, I really appreciated the memorial talk you gave for my momma after she passed. I do ask one favor of you though Sir......please keep 'me' in Your prayers."

"Elvis I am so proud of you. You've been an outstanding citizen and a member of the

"Drug Enforcement Agency" ... "now for awhile, and you know

Elvis... I have always prayed for you. Why you're my 'Bell Ringer' sheep!"

"*Well what's a Bell Ringer Sheep?*" "*Well Elvis, when a shepherd calls to his sheep, one of his sheep has a Bell on him, so when he hears the shepherd's call, he moves. The other sheep follow. They hear the 'bell' on the "Bell Ringer Sheep" and follow him to the shepherd.*

I have hope that one day many will listen
to you as you hopefully will bring the word
of God to them, and you will lead them to the "Great Shepherd," "JESUS CHRIST."

Elvis began to shake and tears flowed from his eyes.
Rex then said, "why Elvis you're shaking,

please, Take my hands." Elvis then took hold of His hands and Rex said, "Let us Pray" After that night, a night neither would forget, Elvis would now believe He had Received a "Spiritual Calling"...one that He would Yearn to fulfill. Would that time ever come?Let us return again to Memphis, I hear the cars all starting to move. The "Funeral Procession" is about to begin...

Chapter 5

"The Funeral Procession"

⌒ↄ

*A*nd so it's time for the Funeral procession...For some, they can't bear to see Elvis' Hearse pass in procession, they cover their eyes to hide their tears. It was indeed a sad day, days none of us, who were alive, and of the age of

understanding back then, will ever forget.

But now we find ourselves here in "77" standing with

thousands of "fans" on "Elvis Presley Blvd., awaiting the funeral procession carrying Elvis' body to his everlasting place of rest.

We hear much whispering. People

are being quiet and yet we hear "voices of despair." We listen in more closely and begin to get the "drift" of the conversation.

I hear one woman speaking loudly, there's no doubt what she is saying. Listen I know you can hear her.

It's a bloody disgrace! It's a bloody disgrace!" I suspect from her accent she's probably from Great Britain.

Wait a minute, another, if I hear him correctly, he too is complaining.

Why couldn't "They" wait 3 or 4 days so some of His fans could be here to pay their respects and wish Him "God Speed."

I tell you readers, this crowd of thousands is not happy with the "Arrangements" at this time. There are other complaints but it's very hard to hear over the thousands who are whispering, it sounds like a muffled "hushing".

But look up ahead, about a couple of hundred yards...it's the "Funeral Procession" everyone's quieting down now, but so many can't keep silent, not being disrespectful, but out of shear grief their sighing, some are moaning others are outright crying their eyes out...

LOOK! LOOK!!... OVER THERE !!!...a women has just fainted. Her child is embracing her, while a man seems to be trying to revive her momma, the little girl is crying also. She's only about 4 years old. My God how sad! She only knows something, something is terribly wrong with her momma she doesn't understand what's going on. Again, another one, and another...

They're falling down all over the place...people are crying...oh so, so sad...so sad.. I'll never forget this day so help me God!

The "Procession is now passing us. OH NO...

a woman just ran up to the Hearse carrying Elvis' body crying and screaming.

A police officer just ran over and pulled her out of harms way. Thank God. He's consoling her at this very moment. I must say these "Memphis" police, and many others from other precincts who are helping out are doing an outstanding Job handling all these people and making sure no one gets hurt. What's that I hear? An elderly woman has just said she heard over her

little "transistor" radio that 2 women have been run
over by cars...I don't know for sure, she seems
a little confused, but wait...I hear another individual
is confirming what she just said...but he says the
2 have died. God help us...it's more than this
crowd can bear. It all seems like a terrible
"Nightmare," so "Unreal" my mind doesn't want me
to believe what I am seeing, but it indeed is real, I
see it with my own two eyes.
I'm beginning to feel faint. It's so hot today...must
be 95 or so, and so stinking humid...
I'm fearful some here will be overcome by the
extreme
heat and humidity...Oh I wish this was over...
I wish I could just wake up and find
it's all been just one Big Bad Nightmare!
Wait, Look! It's here! The "Procession"...
and now it's passing us by and fortunately
we are standing only a couple hundred feet from
the "Mausoleum" where Elvis is to be laid to rest.
I'm told it will be a room not large, but "Gated," and
the coffin will be visible to visitors, but we will
not be
able to enter the room since it's a visually "Open
Vault"
with a gate. I don't know what that means, but when
I get there, I guess I'll understand it better.
Oh...the Hearse has just pulled up to the Mausoleum.
Men are getting out of a number of vehicles.
"Many men" are getting out. They are now opening
the
rear doors of "The Hearse." Everyone is so, so,
quiet now...except for the sighs and muffled sounds of
grief...it seems so..."Unreal." The men who exited from
the other vehicles are now forming 2 lines. I believe

I count....let's see uh...8,...9,.......10,........11...12. Yes it's 6 in each line and the 6 from the one line are facing the 6 from the other line. They are now pulling the casket

from the Hearse. What an unbelievable sight. Just only a few weeks ago I saw Elvis in concert. He was somewhat overweight, but not "grossly." His voice was extraordinary and powerful. How did it all come to this? We're all beside ourselves.

Well the crowds starting to thin out, some are apparently leaving, while some continue to hang on. Maybe they have hopes of seeing the "Casket" inside the Mausoleum.

But I'll just start to head for my vehicle.

Now as I was heading toward my vehicle I saw

four or five people and they seem to be engaged in some serious discussion. The conversation is starting to get loud and a little bit out of control. Let's see if we

can hear what they're saying...

"I tell you 12 or 14 it makes no difference...I'll say it one last time. It should "Not" require that many to carry

that Coffin! Something is not right...and the "viewing" of

his body as he lay in that casket... was something else!

Chapter 6

The Viewing of the Body...
"The Plot Thickens!"

⁓◦⌒

The rest of "That" conversation on that Hot August day of "77," would put me on a 21 year "Search" for "Truth" (?)...

Yes two very "special people" would become an interesting and exciting part of my life. Two people of which "one" would eventually

"Provoke" a change in my life and ...my

"THINKING."

This "provocation" would send me in a "direction" that would have "consequences" beyond belief! Indeed I was to learn an unbelievable "lesson."

Before we journey on I would like to introduce you to these two individuals. I'll use only first names.

The man "Joe Bill" was a distinguished man about 34 years of age. His wife, a woman whose name was

"Becky Sue," was a couple of years younger than he was.

Both of them were from West Virginia. "Joe Bill" was a "Criminal Investigator"...his wife "Becky Sue" was a "Forensic Pathologist."

They both practiced their "professions" in the state of "West Virginia." We developed a very unique friendship over the next few years and would speak to each other by telephone, and communicate by mail. (Snail mail in those days)

Since we lived some 575 miles from each other, this "friendship" would require serious commitment.

Now for the sake of expedience when I refer to "Joe Bill," in this story, I'll use the abbreviation "JB" & when referring to his wife, I'll use "Becky" rather than Becky Sue or her abbreviation ("BS") ... (for obvious reasons) Yes, my "dear reader," on that "Hot August afternoon" so, so long ago, I became part of that "Hot" conversation.

I've never been one to run when the going got tough, and that day would be no exception...

This "relationship" would also "Teach me" what "True Friendship" requires, and the benefits that come from "True Friendships."

Would this "friendship" last? Only "Time" would tell, as "Time" eventually "REVEALS" ALL THINGS!

I would learn "much" over the next 21 years.

For now though, I'd like to take you back to the 17th of August 1977, to relate what I saw when paying my final respects to Elvis and the family.

There were individuals invited as special guests. John Wayne, Ann Margaret, Charley Pride, Burt Reynolds just to name a few.

A very small but "intimate group."

They would be able to view the body, and they were there for the Memorial services conducted by *REX HUMBARD*, a special friend of Elvis and the entire Presley family.

Rex had "Officiated" at the Memorial services for Gladys, Elvis' mother after she had passed away.

From what we were told "Both" services were beautiful. It was at "THIS" Service that Mr. Humbard was told by Vernon to "Recall the episode in Las Vegas" when Rex told Elvis He had hopes that "Elvis would one day lead millions to "Jesus Christ" as Rexes "Bell Ringer Sheep" (This was discussed in chapter 4.)

The services for Elvis were by "Special" invitation only. Since we received no invitation we were unable to attend. (We were his "Fans." And we were not offended one bit, for we knew the family had experienced a tremendous sorrow and loss at Elvis' death. There would only be limited room for guests. Our prayers were with the family and close friends. We were in Memphis for one reason and one reason only, to support Elvis' family.)

Now only a few of us were allowed to view the body and so as we started to pass the casket for viewing, we were told "NO ONE is to take ANY pictures of Elvis as he lay in the casket. Or any other pictures while in line. This line was STRICTLY for viewing and paying our respects to our fallen "Friend" and "Loved One."

Elvis was dressed in a white suite, blue shirt, and white tie.

It was later found out by "JB" that "The National Enquirer" paid a large sum of money to a "cousin" of Elvis who was present at the viewing and would have allowed them to take a picture of Elvis in the casket. Whether that occurred before or after the

"Limited" General viewing, or even before Special guests arrived, we were not able to find out. But the picture was taken and appeared on the front page of "The National Enquirer." This picture would be a real "Shock" to the nation and to many people all over the world. Many felt it was in bad taste, and did not show respect for the tragedy the Presley family was going through. Close friends, and fans, were also suffering.

Yes, this PICTURE would eventually say much. Was the release of this PICTURE to be "Intentional or Unintentional.

If "INTENTIONAL" then for WHAT REASON was it released? To sell papers, or was it to "Send a Message to Someone," or both? We'll DISCUSS this a little later on. But keep this Picture in your memory.

It's also interesting to note that members of a major "Crime Family" from up "North" during the very week that Elvis "died," were being indicted for criminal acts that involved "Drug trafficking." "JB" discovered this in the summer of 83 while doing criminal investigating for The State of West Virginia.

State Troopers were running into some drug traffickers up and down the West Virginia Interstate, especially during the summer racing season. This would be brought to my attention by "JB" in the winter of 1983 when "JB" and Becky visited me in Memphis.

But for now, let's return to the viewing line as we proceed in single file, to pay our last respects to Elvis, his family and close friends.

As we are moving closer and closer to the casket, we hear some muffled conversation. The people are very quite, but there seems to be some whispering going on. Let's listen in carefully...I think this may be important since the crowd is getting a little noisy.

OH, Oh... the crowd is now being asked to "simmer it down."

I am now coming up to the casket, I can't see him yet, I'm a bit short and so many are much taller than I am. I must admit although it is a blistering 95 degrees outside and heavy humidity it's absolutely refreshing in here. They have the air conditioning on Full Blast! Those air conditioning blowers must be set at Maximum speed and the stand up fans are enormous, but they are keeping the place cool. Unfortunately though, one can hardly hear oneself in here. (It's a bit noisy)

With all those blowers on and the whispering its Hard to even think right now, but who cares, we're out of that stinking heat and humidity let those cool blowers make all the NOISE they want to make. I feel cool.

.... OH, OH, here we are, we're now passing the casket, yes, I can see him!

OH, how sad it is. Wait a minute, what is that I see? Apparently others are seeing it also. It looks as if Elvis is perspiring, just below his hairline. That's strange....and what is "THAT" I see?.....It's his sideburns. It appears that one is "lifted" off his face. Could it be he had fake sideburns all these years?.... NO, I've seen him in person many times and close up. I've been the leader of one of his largest fan clubs in the world. I've been privileged to see him even "backstage"... no something's wrong. It looks like someone "GLUED" his sideburns on and didn't do such a good job. And now as I pear at his "NOSE" it too looks odd...a bit "PUDGY"...Elvis had a "PROMINENT" nose, and now as I look a bit closer "This Elvis" seems to be a Much YOUNGER looking Elvis, why LOOK AT HIS HANDS, they look so soft and extremely SMOOTH. How can that be? After all Elvis practiced karate and I remember when I saw him backstage after one of his concerts in "77" his hands were Rough probably from all those karate chops, and breaking wood, bricks, blocks and whatever else he could break. When he shook my hand that evening I could feel the coarseness in his hands. ...I wonder if that is Really him in that casket? Maybe they have the real corpse somewhere else for "security" purposes.

I don't know... This just seems so unreal, the entire situation.

"OK, OK, I hear you, yes I'll move along".....
(Apparently I'm holding the line up, taking too
   much time viewing the casket.) Well that
   was my day on the 17th of August 1977.
   It was indeed a day I would never forget. Thankfully,
I'm happy to say I was able to recall
   most of what I saw. For it would play a big role in my
"search for the truth."

⌒୨

Chapter 7

"Sightings & points to consider"

∽

So here we are back again in 1977. It's been about 2 months, and "strange" things begin to happen.

We are now hearing reports of "sightings" of Elvis.... In Kalamazoo, California, Tennessee and other parts of the country. I was a fairly young man in those days and those "sightings" were viewed as being ridiculous. The "World" all knew Elvis had died. And so it became a bit of a "Joke."

Whenever something unusual would happen at someone's place of employment or any place at all, someone would inevitably say, "yeah, and I heard on my car radio this morning someone saw Elvis at McDonalds," or Elvis was sighted at Burger King. Yes Elvis sightings were "popping" up in some of the strangest places.

As time would move on we would hear "Elvis was seen at other locations, shopping centers restaurants, the post office, working in a hotel, and it would go on and on.

I distinctly remember going to an "Elvis Review Concert."

The Review Concert Elvis impersonator doing "Elvis" was really pretty good!

Of course there were a number of Elvis fans in the audience, many were dressed like Elvis...hair, sunglasses, raised lip and some even had Elvis Jumpsuits, not exactly like Elvis but similar. They would imitate him when they would speak, and some would do a pretty good imitation of Elvis. Inevitably, there would be someone, who would "stand out more outstandingly" than all those impersonators, and so there was said to be an "Elvis Sighting" at that very concert.

Most of us just laughed it off and remained with big grins on our faces, ignoring the "foolishness" of the so-called "sighting".

Who in their right mind would believe Elvis was "walking among us!" This became a big thing, kind of a part of "American Culture." "The sightings of Elvis Presley," yet everyone "knew" it was always a joke.

People were just "Funnin."

⌒⊙

Now let's change our direction for a moment as we now consider a few points.

"JB" was in communication with me and he said he had some thoughts we should discuss concerning our "search."

To do so, he said, would require us to review some details about 8/16/77.

According to "JB," One of the Oldest Presley Fan Club's presidents contacted Vernon Presley after hearing the news of Elvis' "death."

She was told she should not come to Memphis until "Next week." He said it was too hectic, too many people. Members of the Presley family were coming and that would include many, he just felt it would be better if she came a week later since things would be less hectic.

"JB" told me this was a "clue" concerning Elvis' so called "faked death." What he meant wasn't explained to me at that time. JB" also pointed to another supposed "clue," that stood out to fans. This was the "misspelling" of Elvis middle name on his grave marker.

"JB" found out Elvis spelt his middle name with one "A".... Aron.

It had been legally changed from 2 "A" s to one "A" at Elvis' birth. So then His name on his birth certificate was spelt with one "A." His high school Diploma with one "A". His marriage license with one "A." His Army papers with one "A." His contracts with one "A".

Why did Vernon spell his son's name with two "A's?" on his grave marker?" ...This would also add to the puzzle. Would Elvis be happy with his name "Misspelled" on his Grave marker? I don't think so... how would you feel? "Jb" stated Elvis faked his death and since Elvis was superstitious, He had His name "misspelled" on the Grave Marker so as not to "Tempt Fate." It appeared "JB" had some good points, or *so it seemed.*

Another very serious matter "JB" brought to my attention had to do with where Elvis was supposedly buried.

Originally his coffin was placed in the Memphis Mausoleum, in a small room "gated and locked."

We were then told that individuals tried to "steal the coffin" with the corpse in it, and so it was decided to bury Elvis at "Graceland" after the proper permits would be issued. When I returned to Graceland, after Elvis was buried, I was totally taken back when I saw where they placed him. It was always Elvis' wishes to be buried "Next to His Mother," *or so we thought.* **Those wishes were not granted I asked myself.... WHY? ...** *Again "JB" seemed to have a "valid" point.* **Then "JB" mentioned the body in the coffin. He claimed it was not Elvis but a waxed figure of him and the coffin had a refrigeration unit within it to keep the wax figure from "Melting" on that hot august day. He said the noise from the compressor in the coffin would be a problem due to it's noise level.** *I told him when I viewed the "Body" I could not hear myself "think" much less hear any "noise" from A Compressor in the coffin.* **There was so much noise at Graceland with Fans running, A.C. units blowing cold air at high speeds drowning out any sound from anywhere. "JB" said that's exactly why "THEY" had the fans and A.C. units blowing at full speed, to drown out any noise. Well** *it seemed to make sense to me since I didn't believe it was Elvis in that casket from the way he looked.*

Time would eventually "Lay bare" what had been covered over...*or was it "covered over?"*

Now our "Journey" begins to speed up as we now cover a point concerning a "decision" Elvis would make. One that He would live to sadly regret I believe.

Chapter 8

"Elvis"

"Federal Agent at Large"

⎯⎯⌒⌒⎯⎯

*I*t was widely known by many, that Elvis had been involved in "Law Enforcement" on a local level, although he had been given "Honorary" authority in many states. It was then in December 1970, while en route to Washington D.C. by air, and in the presence of a noted Senator that Elvis wrote "Then President Richard M. Nixon," explaining his concern for the Nation and the problems at work in the illegal "proliferation" and "trafficking" of Drugs. He would then request a meeting with President Nixon to "Discuss" the problem and how He could possibly be of assistance.

Elvis then told The President He had spoken to The Vice President one week ago while in Palm Springs and expressed His concerns for the country, the drug culture, the Hippie elements, the SDS, the Black Panthers, etc.

He explained to The President that these groups did not consider Him to be a threat. Elvis then said He could and would be of any service to help the country out. He also expressed that He had no ulterior motives.

It would be his wish not to be given a "Title," or an "Appointed position." Elvis felt He could do more by remaining a federal agent at large. He could use His communication and connections with people of all ages to be of help, in tracking down these formenters of trouble. He then told The President that He would be staying at the Washington Hotel in room 505, 506, & 507, registered as Jon Burrows.

The two would meet at Washington D.C. in The "Presidential Oval Office" in the "White House," and arrangements would be made for Elvis to be trained so as to act as a "Federal Agent at Large."

It wasn't long after this that Jack Anderson of "The Washington Post" would write an article about Elvis becoming a Federal Agent at Large. This put everything "out front."

In my opinion, this put Elvis in a very dangerous position. From approximately 1974-76 Elvis provided cover for an undercover agent who posed as a member of Elvis' band. There would eventually be assassination threats to Elvis' life, as FBI reports would document.

Elvis knew the danger that would exist, but little did He realize the danger He would eventually have to face.

But "fear" was something foreign to this man! In fact "Fear,' was NO part of his Vocabulary.

As "William Earnest Henley" once wrote... The "Coward" dies a thousand deaths, but "The Valiant" taste of death but once!".... And Elvis was indeed a "Valiant" Man.

I seriously believe this decision to be a
Part of the D.E.A. would become His "Waterloo." (That which would "Break Him.")

In 1990 after conversing with "JB" for about 2 weeks, we decided to look a little Deeper into the "Federal Agent at Large" Deal.

Remember at this time we were looking into something that was better than 10 years in the past. "JB" had made numerous phone calls through the years to me but the call that came in "92" seemed to be different, very different.

"JB" had connections in high places. So in March of "92" I received a phone call from him. He said we needed to see each other "Eye to Eye." So we set a date and met in Nashville. It was a 5-hour drive for me from Memphis and for "JB" 5 hours from West Virginia. Nashville was the location for the meetings we would have, and we had many.

"JB'S wife "Becky," the "Forensic pathologist," had been involved with the Search for "Truth" right from the beginning. She would accompany "JB" whenever we would meet in Nashville. She was such a "Pleasant" woman.

She uncovered a Number of important parts of the "puzzle."

The death certificate of Elvis and the Letter he wrote to President Nixon.

After careful examination she found out

That it "appeared" Elvis may have filled out His own death certificate. Having secured a copy of the death certificate and having it Analyzed by three different hand writing analysts, comparing the death certificate with the letter he wrote President Nixon...the results...

We found all 3 analysts agreed. Who ever

Wrote the letter to President Nixon also filled out the death certificate.

To us this was a big breakthrough. It "Seemed" Elvis may have "faked" his own death. But was this enough? We shall see, but something very unusual was about to happen, very unusual...

Chapter 9

"One Candle..."

⌒◯

*I*t was now August 15th 1995. Elvis had been
gone 18 years.
Memphis was aglow with visitors from all over the
world. It was August 15, 1995, and people came from
everywhere or so it seemed to memorialize the "passing" of Elvis.
Oh yes it was to be a day for:
The "Candlelight Vigil,"
which would begin at sunset and continue
through the night until the early hours of the 16th.
Music was softly playing, people were milling
around "Hawkers" were selling their wares to the
fans.
I must say for a day of "reflection" on one man's
life, it seemed to me that everyone was enjoying
themselves.

But as night fell, I was taken back by the shear mass
of humanity that joined in the "candlelight vigil" that
evening.

The candles lit up all around me, my little candle seemed so "insignificant," I mentioned it to a gentleman standing next to me.

He smiled and said...... *"Does not one candle in a room full of "Darkness" make a bright light?"*

I thought for a moment and replied, "yes... it does...yes...it...does"

He then said.... "Sometimes <u>too much light</u> can be <u>blinding.</u>"

I stayed there through the "vigil with my little candle in my hand. That stranger seemed "friendly" but I felt a little uneasy in his presence, why? ...I don't know.

Anyway, after the vigil the crowds dispersed.

But all throughout the evening into the wee hours of morning there was much to see and especially "hear."

As a fan of Elvis I wanted to "Do what I felt was Right as respects his Name & Legacy."

To me it meant being there to

keep the "memory alive."

I felt I was a small part of a *"bigger picture."*

Kinda like that "little candle" *I held the previous night.*

By itself *it gave little light, "together" with all those Elvis Fans it* Contributed *to a much Bigger and Brighter Light."*

I guess that "stranger" gave me some food for thought. He did seem happy. I wish I had gotten his name.... Oh well...what difference would it make, he probably was from out of state anyhow.

"friendfromyesteryear"

Yeah another "JB" probably!

What's wrong with me? I'm starting to sound like those people who were screaming at "JB" the day of Elvis' funeral back in "77."

I better take a chill pill!

I was hoping "JB" and "Becky Sue" would be here this year, but according to "JB," he & "Becky Sue" would not be able to make it since they had "pressing" business.

It seemed like something was happening to our "friendship."
This was the 5th straight year they were unable to make it. We began seeing less and less of each other, and now with computers around we resorted to e-mails to keep in touch. I wasn't that savvy when it came to computers, so staying in touch became harder.

"JB" would send me information on some investigating he had completed that was in reference to our "search" for the "Truth" about Elvis' death. But I started to become a little discouraged when he would place "attachments" and "files" that required downloading in his e-mails. All that computer jazz was foreign to me, and made my job very difficult. "JB" suggested I take a course in computer fundamentals. That was easy for him to say but I had little money.
I worked as a pickup truck driver for a small electrical contractor in Memphis.
The pay was meager to say the least, and
I was barely getting along.

Meanwhile "JB" & his wife" Becky" were doing
Well with their careers. I had been to their home
once in 1990 and it was absolutely magnificent. Five
bedrooms, 4 baths, formal dining room, fireplaces (2),
tennis courts, in ground swimming pool, and "domes-
tics" to care for their Estate. All on 25 acres in beautiful
West Virginia.

"Me," I live in *a rented room* in Memphis.

"It works for me!"

The next day I decided to treat myself to breakfast
"out." No hot plate cook top for me today! It was only
a 20 minute walk to the "fast food" restaurant and I
was going to treat myself to a "Big Breakfast." Yep, I
deserved it! Especially after attending such a beautiful
memorial service!

Why not continue the celebration!!!

When I arrived at the restaurant I marched up to
that counter and told that young boy, "I want a Big
Breakfast!"
I know it's probably no big thing to ya'll but to
me... this was the "Cats Meow."

Let me tell you I really enjoyed that meal!

After dumping my tray of trash I turned and whom
did I see walking out of the restaurant but the man I
had seen the night before at the candle light vigil?
The "stranger."

His words repeated in my ears...

"Does *not one candle in a room full of "Darkness"*
make a bright light?"

"Sometimes too much light can be blinding."

I just stood there motionless, ...thinking...

Chapter 10

"Christmas at Graceland"

...1996

⎯◦

*I*t was December of 1996, "Graceland" and Memphis were aglow with the Christmas Spirit, tinsel, Poinsettias, garland, Christmas Trees, holly, mistletoe, and Christmas songs everywhere you went. (All sung by Elvis...of course!)

People were joyous, enjoying the season and of course most were awaiting the 25ᵗʰ.

I've always had a good "sense of humor" and so I decided to make this Christmas "special."

I now began the "Enormous Project" of getting my rented "One Room" into the "Holiday Spirit."

There were "Christmas cards" on my wall, only two, so I decided to treat myself by buying Christmas cards and sending them to myself.

My landlord was impressed at the 75 cards I received from various people.

(People I made up)

May God forgive me it was Christmas and here I was sinning!...

Everyone received many cards, but I received only two. So I had to do something.

I intended to make this Christmas a "special" one by inviting some friends over.

Now a "one rented room" would not exactly allow for a "Concert" Size Crowd. So I had to choose my guests very carefully.
1. My Mother 2. My Father

We had ourselves a "Big Time."
What better friends could there be than one's parents for Christmas dinner!
I really went out for this one and had the Event "Catered." (For all 3 of us) It was a Big Surprise when momma and Dad were sitting down and all of sudden there came a knocking at my door!

The "Caterer" had arrived!!

I asked momma if she would please answer the door. What a surprise when she opened it and there stood my "Caterer."

He boldly declared, "I have 3 Pepperoni Pizzas, steaming hot and just made!"

Well, my momma likely fell over with laughter.

Dad just looked at me, shook his head and smiled.

Yes sirrreee we had it "Catered just like those rich folks do." And it was "GRAND."

I know dad and mom were proud of me, they said I handled the occasion beautifully!

After dinner we took our customary walk over to "Graceland" to see all the beautiful lights, and decorations. In fact while we were there gazing about it began to snow. Just lightly but a continuous snowfall. How pretty it was.

We took some pictures with dad's camera, he said he would pay for the developing, I insisted that I should pay but dad was quite firm in his convictions and so he handled it.

Graceland had "Elvis Recordings" of Christmas songs playing all through the holiday. It was absolutely a very uplifting and joyous evening. And so we continued walking around and listening to the music.

As usual for these events there is always a "crowd" to see the "Christmas Tree and lit grounds around Graceland."

We as usual would not be the only ones there. Many others were also enjoying the "festivities."

And so we stood looking at the lights as people mingled in the crowd.

It was starting to get a little cold and I knew mom and dad were starting to catch a chill.

Just about then I felt someone ever so gently tapping me on my shoulder. I turned and as I did to my surprise it was the "Stranger" I saw back in August at the candle light vigil, and the same person I saw when I went out for that "Big Breakfast" and now here he was again and he was smiling. A very warm smile. An almost "How have you been smile?" I was beside myself. I didn't know what to say. He said..

"Merry Christmas" to me and then turned to my mom and dad and shook dad's hand and gave my momma a gentle hug wishing them both a merry Christmas. As he started to walk away he turned and looked at me and said with a smile,

"We will meet again, I look forward to it."

I cried out *"What's your name?* He said in a very soft tone... *"friend"*

And disappeared into the crowd."

My dad turned to me and said, "son how is it you know this man?" I was just standing there mesmerized at what just happened. My momma turned to me and said,

"Jesse" my son...

Didn't you hear your daddy?
Who was that man?"
I answered....... "friend.......?"

Chapter 11

January 7, 1997

∽◯

"*1996*" *seemed to fly by and here we were in a New Year. It was January 7, 1997. Had Elvis lived, tomorrow He would have been 62 years old. Old enough to collect "early social security benefits." But we all knew He had "left us"*

20 years ago.

As usual there were "great crowds" all over Memphis. The restaurants were full, traffic was heavy but the Memphis police kept everything running smooth. Elvis fans were polite, they seemed to share a common goodness during these events.

People would arrive from all over the world. Greet each other on the streets, a cheerful smile was evident on their faces. If you were a fan of Elvis, you were considered a "friend" to "them." And So it went.

These celebrations, His "death," Elvis Week, Christmas at Graceland, and the celebration of His birth, had become annual events. We all looked forward to them with eager anticipation. Yes we knew Elvis was no longer with us, but it appeared at these gatherings that the same "spirit" of helping, sharing, greeting one another with a smile, *"the spirit Elvis had shown when He was with us,"* was without a doubt present with us now. And so the celebrations took on a very warm atmosphere, an atmosphere of... *"Love."*

Yes He was *"gone,"* and yet *"still"* with us.

My search for the *"Truth"* as to Elvis' demise would soon come to an *emotional end.*

This *"search"* would teach me a valuable lesson but this lesson would be accompanied with *much pain.* It would be the loss of someone *"I thought was my friend"....* But my *"love for Elvis,"* *"the man,"* and *"Respect" for the "Presley Name,"* would lead me to something of *"Exceedingly Greater Value."*

Chapter 12

A "Friendship?"... Ends!

❧

*I*t was in 1998 that I received a call from "Old JB." It had been a few years since we spoke. He was very excited, I can still hear his voice clearly as we spoke...

"Jesse, I have some real Big news for you.

But I cannot talk to you over the phone about this, we need an "eye to eye" discussion. I'm sure you'll have questions. We can meet in Nashville but we'll have to be careful. *The "Shadows" are following me."*

"The *"shadows,"* what are you talking about?"

"I can't speak about this over the phone. Can we meet in Nashville this week at our usual spot?"

"What day, today's Wednesday?"

"How about this, Saturday at 4:00P.M.?"

"O.K." Saturday will be fine. But there's one prob-lem. You know I have no Vehicle to travel in. All these meetings we have had over some 21 years to discuss what we both have found in this "search" has required

me to borrow a vehicle from someone each time we met. So although the day to meet is fine, it's going to have to be in Memphis
at that "fancy Restaurant" in town
and you can buy me dinner....
How's that sound to you?

O.K. Jesse, but this is really "Big" news I'm sure you will be impressed. See you on Saturday in Memphis 4:00 P.M.

Well that conversation would be the beginning of the end of our friendship.
When Saturday came I headed out to the restaurant in Memphis. This meeting would not be an "as usual" meeting anymore, being a number of years had passed with no phone calls thus no meetings.

Now at 4:15 JB walks in. He's late. Becky Sue is not with Him. That's unusual since She has always been with Him whenever we met for discussion.
Anyway we are here, now what? I would soon understand JB's intentions.
Let's not forget He and "Becky Sue" had missed some 5 or 6 years of "Celebration" in Memphis. This to me was not good since we all
Loved Elvis or so I thought.

And so the conversation began.
"Hi Jesse it's been awhile. I have a question for you. You've been living in "Memphis" all your life. I'm sure you have some contacts who can help "us" with some publicity."
Publicity for what?
Well I've gathered enough information now to throw serious doubt on Elvis' being dead. I want to write a

Book, a "Tell All" story....it will set Memphis on "Fire!
It can throw out all kinds of "Dirt."
We can make a fortune!

Set "Memphis" on fire? Make a fortune? What are
you nuts? This was supposed to be a "curiosity search"
in hopes that Elvis Made it "out" and has been able
to enjoy a life out from under the spotlight..nothing
more!

Look Jesse let's calm down, how about a drink?
No...
Well I'm going to have a little whiskey. "WAITER!"....
yes sir...a double shot of Jack Daniels Green please...
"coming up."

At this point I was ready to walk out, but instead I
decided to pose a question to "JB."
So how's "Becky Sue" doing? How come she's not
with you?
"Didn't I call you about her?"
"No," you haven't called in a dogs age...(JB. now
lays his head down on the table and begins to speak...
he's sobbing)

We were so involved in the "Search" that Becky
Sue didn't have time to go for her annual Physical for
some 6 years. We were just so busy wrapped up in the
"Search."
"Becky Sue came down with cancer 4 years ago and
she passed away last year."
What?
I really loved her Jesse...
"Are you kidding me? You didn't make her get her
annual physical? What's wrong with you? And then you

never called me? I could of at least helped console her
during her last days."

I'm sorry Jesse it was just one of those things.

"One of those things, What things?
I'll tell you what things "JB" ...*you were <u>too busy</u>*
<u>making money to care about Becky's health</u> and you
never had the <u>decency</u> to inform me about Becky's condition. I would have
<u>borrowed the money, to fly out to see Her!</u>"

"Please Jesse hear me out what Becky Sue and I
found out *will make us both "Rich."*

"Rich? You've always been rich. How much more do you want you greedy
$.O.B.? **I told you back in "77" I was just curious, it was**
you who put these "Stupid ideas" in my head. Elvis
faked His death, wax corpse in the casket, no flag
draped coffin, faked Death Certificate's, Numerology,
mispelling of his midle name on gravesite, Gravesite
location of Elvis body. What other "BS" do you have?"
I'm not going to get involved in a witch-hunt!

"JB," it's not our business!
Elvis gave His "ALL" right to the end!

If He died, what *<u>pain of "Heart"</u>* **we would be**
bringing on his *<u>family</u>* **rehashing issues**
that only <u>cause pain.</u>
"JB" LET IT GO! There's nothing good that can
come from this.
What "if" He really had to fake his death?
What if the "Threats" were real?
If you could "Prove it" what would you actually be
doing?

You would give cause for Evil Ones to try to find him and do Him harm!

It's WRONG!

So help me, if you write a book that Disrespects His family or causes any harm to "Anyone related" I will personally come for you...have you got it!

NOW GO!!!

This conversation is over, I'm sorry I ever got involved in that conversation back in "77".

And so ended a "friendship" that dragged along for 21 years. A waste of time and energies.

While I was "Searching for Truth" my friend was Searching for "A Pot of Gold." What's worse, He had no morals.

He had no "compassion" for the Presley family."

He was selfish and cared only for himself, while millions of fans worldwide grieved, and suffered emotional pain, *not even Elvis' Daughter, "Lisa Marie" would "JB" spare. She, who had the misfortune of growing up without her daddy.* **Yes, fans of Elvis are known for their desire to "Protect the Image and Reputation" of Elvis Presley and the Presley family.**

I felt so bad at what could have happened had "JB" wrote that book with nothing but conjecture, and "hearsay." And who knows if *so called pieces of "evidence" were "Faked" and Elvis death being the "reality?"*

"Time would tell."

Chapter 13

"Does not one candle in a darkened room make a Bright Light?" ... "friend"

∾⊙

Now I was not aware that sitting at a dining table with 3 of his associates only 4 tables away from us was "friend." After "JB" left the table and the restaurant, "friend" walked slowly over to my table. As I looked up at him he looked at me very solemnly. As He spoke, His words would resonate in my brain....

"Does not one candle in a darkened room make a bright light?"..."Too much light can be "Blinding."

Then "friend" looked at me for a moment and "Smiled."

I *now* understood!

We had enough "Light" with that one candle, "Elvis," to "see" & hear all He had left us.

On the other hand to search for what is not for us to know or any of our business to know is to search for a "Light" that blinds us causing us to <u>loose our focus</u>

as to what a "Great Treasure" and "Legacy" we have found and been given to enjoy and it comes "Free of Charge."

How sad to not recognize what is truly valuable in life. Elvis knew it, and it all stemmed around

"love of God and Neighbor"....

He sang about it so many times....for who?....To praise His Lord & for us to enjoy the sense of "Peace" these songs were meant to give.

Take a moment "Reader" and listen to him sing,

"If I can Dream"

"Yes," God Blessed" the poor boy from Tupelo who gained "The Riches" few ever find in life....a "Strong Relationship" with his "Creator" as it manifested itself in His Music and the love He showed for all, including but not limited to, His fans, charities, helpless children, and strangers whom He never knew, and yet He would make their

"dreams come true!"

As time moved on I would see things that would make me more aware of how Elvis' Life was "moving others" in a very positive way. It was as though He were still with us.

One event I will never forget occurred on January 8th of that year (Elvis Birthday) at a local restaurant where a Mother and her 4 children were having dinner.

Well apparently this poor soul did not have enough money to pay the bill. By her facial expression I could tell she was embarrassed. But shortly, there appeared a man who took the waiter over into a corner, away from the woman.

The stranger then looked at the bill and whispered to the waiter. The waiter then went over to the woman and as he was handing the bill to the woman before she was able to take it he tore it up. The woman was unbelievably surprised. Apparently the stranger said something to the waiter, in any case her debt was discharged.

I didn't want anyone to see me "staring" but as I cautiously watched, the stranger left the restaurant immediately after speaking to the waiter, so the woman never had a chance to thank him.

I'm sure she didn't know him, for he left without saying anything to her. What a kindness!

After the stranger left he continued to walk over to his car. But in doing so his steps would take him right pass the window I was sitting next to.

As he passed our eyes made contact. To my surprise it was "friend!"

I was so happy, for it was "friend" who had helped that poor woman and her children. It just made me so happy!

He appeared to be in a hurry, so although I couldn't speak with him as he passed the window where I sat I gave him a quick "Thumbs Up" and as He passed by He smiled and held his hand out "pointing to me" in a gesture of friendship.

There just seemed to be something "special" about him that I couldn't put my finger on.

On another occasion while riding on the bus during one of the annual Elvis celebrations I saw a vehicle on the side of the road.

A women was trying to change her tire since it had gone flat...you'll never guess who showed up while our bus was stopped for a red light. Or maybe you've already figured it out.

Yes, you're correct, it was "friend."

I began to think, "This guy is like "Superman," when there's a problem, up "pops" "friend."

Now I say this not to be critical of "friend," but it was indeed "strange," to say the least. He seemed to be there whenever someone needed help. It made me think of the many times Elvis would be there to Help people. How did "friend" know, or was it just coincidence, or was he just someone who saw a problem and was *willing to help.*

In any case to me, "friend" was a "prince."

Chapter 14

Elvis... a very "Generous Soul"

~⁀~

E lvis would do concerts to raise money for some worthy cause. At one point in time, "Elvis" was supporting "fifty" Charities in "Memphis" alone. One such worthy cause is St. Jude's Children's Hospital in Memphis, built as a "Lifetimes Work" of the late Comedian/actor Danny Thomas.

St. Jude's Children's Hospital specializes in the treatment and cures for childhood cancers, and has a policy that guarantees "No Child is turned away" due to lack of ability to pay for life saving care. What a wonderful organization! Mr. Danny Thomas' daughter Marlo Thomas has carried the "Torch" since her Father's passing, indeed another sweetheart who has been loyal to her daddy's "Cause."

There have been many charities Elvis supported. Take a trip to "Graceland" and you will see some of the organizations Elvis so generously supported. It's "Unbelievable how much money this Man gave to charity, "Millions", and that same spirit of giving continues to manifest itself with the "Presley" family and E.P.E. The "Legend" continues on, The "fairytale continues to be told."

In the same "Spirit of Giving" a portion of any profits from this book will be donated to Various Charities.

"Motto," never "Take more than you give." (makes sense doesn't it!)

Elvis would probably say anyone who would try to profit off His name for unjust gain would have to answer to "The Almighty." (?)

My deepest respect to Miss Lisa Marie, but Elvis was not making that statement about Her, (although I know she is a staunch supporter for her Daddy..) but rather He was alluding to "Almighty God."

There are millions of "Fans" that will stand to protect the Name, Legend, and unforgettable history of "The poor boy from Tupelo" who rose from nothing to become one of, if not, the "Best," of all time recording artists, "Loving Father," Son, and Philanthropist.

Amazingly, Despite His Fame and fortune, Elvis Never forget his heritage, or where He came from nor did He ever feel "Superior" to anyone. Certainly He was a fine example of a man we all would of loved to have had as a "friend."

We the fans appreciate that and will do all we can to assist in any way we can. Yes, "God Blessed," The "poor boy" from Tupelo."

༄

My search for the truth as to "Elvis demise" would soon come to an end. I would become "Privileged," to know the "Truth" as to what really happened on 8/16/77.

"JB." was out of my life, and sadly "Becky Sue" had "passed on." I was informed that in January of 2000 "JB" also passed on. Sadly He lost His life when His Private Plane went down in a bad storm. friends of his said He had a "Secret Manuscript," he was heading up North to speak with a publisher about. They said He wouldn't reveal it's subject or contents to anyone.

Well obviously He never accomplished

"Publishing the Book." I was not happy over His passing but I was "relieved" He never published that "TRASH."

What a sad waste of some 21 years and "loosing" ones "Life" in the Process.

It brings to mind another verse from God's word that Elvis often quoted from. It went something like this..."Of what Benefit is it for a man to gain all the "Riches" this world has to offer but to loose his life in the process."

I truly believe that is one very important reason why Elvis saw "Fame and Fortune" as "passing things of no lasting value." In The Song He sang "Fame & "Fortune." His "words" explain what He truly felt was of value. Stop and listen to a recording of it if at all possible, before continuing on in this story. It will really "Move Your Heart."

A verse from "fame"& "fortune" simply states,..

"fame & fortune" how empty they can be, but when I hold you in my arms that's Heaven to me." (Yes it's "LOVE" that brings with it "Everlasting Superlative Riches.") Listen to Elvis sing "Never Ending Love.".......beautifully expresses the True sentiment of "Love."

I too was to experience another quality of "Love."

Yes My "love" for Elvis, "the man," and "Respect" for The "Presley Name" would allow me to experience the quality of "Love" in a way I never imagined.

Stay with me, you're in for a Surprise!

Chapter 15

Jesse sees another aspect of Elvis'

"Generosity"

⌒♥

One day I was taking a "Guided Tour" of Graceland. Our "Guide" for the group was introducing himself to us when he was interrupted by another Guide who said politely "take a break," I'll take "THIS" group.

Who was our Guide now? A somewhat short man but as He came closer I recognized it was "friend."

He took me out of the back of the crowd and brought me to the front of the line telling the guests I was someone very "special," he had known for years and He didn't want to loose me.

ME?...Someone "Special" to "friend?" At
This point my curiosity was busting at the seems!

He didn't want to loose me?

What did He mean by that?

And so now I began putting all these "chance" meetings to question.

"What" I would soon come to understand would change my life forever!

It now was "Springtime" in Beautiful Tennessee. The year was 2001. Although our Beautiful Tennessee was undergoing the changes of "Springtime," beautiful colorful flowers, flowering trees, dogwoods, redbuds, etc. my "heart" was in deep sadness over the passing of my Mother in September of 2000, and also the passing of my Father in December of 2000. I was a sure missing them. I still do. Other than that my life had not changed much. I was now in my 48ᵗʰ year of life. I was still living in my rented room, still working for that small electrical contractor driving that same old pickup truck. I still could not afford a vehicle and my legs were starting to bother me. So walking to work although only about a quarter mile became difficult.

One Saturday while taking a short walk into town I started "window shopping" at the auto dealerships. Boy those new cars sure looked nice.

But it was only a dream for me, a new car was out of my "league," but an old piece of "Junk" would be right up my alley.

As I continued to gaze through the Dealership windows I saw a beautiful 2001 Powder Blue "Cadillac" convertible. I was "oblivious" to pedestrians walking up and down the sidewalk in Memphis, being "mesmerized" by that beautiful vehicle, when all of a sudden I felt a "Tap" on my shoulder.

As I turned around who was standing there? It was "friend" and He said to me...

"She sure looks Beautiful, doesn't she?"

I just smiled.

He then said, "Come on, follow me."

And so I followed him into the Dealership. We walked up to that Cadillac and "friend" said...

"Sit in it." I told him,

"No thanks, I have my old work cloths on, I don't belong sitting in this kinda vehicle dressed like this."

"friend" then turned to the Salesman and said, "Can he sit in it?"....

The salesman replied,

"Of course "friend," whatever you want to do."

"friend" then said, "Jesse get in that car!"

Well I tell you I was a hopping into that vehicle..."Weeeeeeeeeeh!"

"You like it?"

"SHE'S a Dream!"

Then "friend" really shocked the "pants" off of me when He said.. "Jesse it's no dream, SHE'S yours!"

Tommy get Her ready for Jesse. Put the insurance on it. I'll bring you my check when we pick it up."

Oh that's O.K. "friend" no rush on the check your credit is good here."

"We'll pick it up this afternoon and Tommy make good darn sure that vehicle "Sparkles" when we pick it up. Got it?"

"Yes "SIR" Mr. "friend"

Jesse top "up" or "down" when we pick it up?

Well "friend" the weathers beautiful I'd like the "Top" down, if that's OK with you."

Jesse it's your vehicle, any way YOU want it.

"Top Down!"(Jesse)

….Hear Him Tommy?"

"Yes sir Mr. "friend" Top Down!"

"I had a hard time believing this was happening to me. It was like a "fairytale"…..It didn't seem real, but I tell you this, when "friend" and I met later that afternoon to pick that "Baby" up, there she was a "Gleaming and a Shining." I said to "friend" "God Bless you "friend." He politely replyed, "you're welcome".

I tell you She was no "Fairytale."

This "drop top" Cadillac was baby "Blue." What a sight! "Wheew!" And Mr. Tommy the salesman had the top "DOWN."

"friend" and I spent the rest of the day driving around Memphis and into the country. The weather was beautiful and so "friend" and I had a great time! He later took me out to dinner at the same restaurant I saw Him pay for that lady and Her 4 children. I felt improperly dressed but "friend" assured me not to be concerned I was his "guest."

When we said goodnight he asked me how much gas was left in the car. I told him it looks like it's a little under a quarter of a tank.

"Go to the nearest gas station and fill her up!" (I had 3 dollars in my pocket, and so I told him)

"Don't be concerned, we'll use my credit card."
And so when I got to the gas station He handed me his credit card. I told the attendant to, fill "HER" up!

That sounded strange to me. After he filled "HER" up I handed him "friend's" credit card.

He looked at it, then looked at My spanking New Caddy and said, "wowee..... *"The Inner Circle!"*

I had no Idea of what he was saying and so I asked "friend" what did that "Inner Circle" mean? He just smiled and said:
"does not one candle in a dark room make a bright light?"
... Sometimes
"Too much light can be "Blinding."

I left it at that, and went home that night to my "one room" rental. What happened on Monday when I showed up for work is another story, my landlord's eyes almost popped out of her head when she saw my "gift" and that's exactly what I told both my Employer on Monday and my Landlord that night,

"it was a "Gift" From a.....

"friend"

Chapter 16

"Consequences"

~⌒~

*S*o I went to bed that night, so excited at what had transpired that day. Still totally amazed at what a generous man "friend" really was.

I remember hearing about Elvis' generosity, many years ago as I had been living in Memphis all my life. His generosity was and still is "Legendary." He never advertised it, but the "locals" would speak of it based on many occasions where those who told, were those who had received. So these were not "fairytales" although most of those who received the benefit of Elvis generosity often couldn't believe it was happening to them. But it was.

Now I know "friend" was not "Elvis." Why? A couple of things. I'll whisper... *"friend" was too S*HORT.*"*

Another point about "friend" is that he was *a little Chunky"*. Now I'm not trying to be disrespectful to "friend" he was a great human being.

I couldn't help but wonder what his "real" name was?

From what he said I guess it was *not for me to know, or at least not at that time.* So being *a contented individual* I accepted *what was and it sufficed. Little did I know that one day "friend" would not only explain why he was called "friend" but also what the "significance" of that "name" really "meant." Yes these were things I would eventually come to know.*

Surprises were in store for me as time would march on, and surprises that would answer questions I had about Elvis' death would also be answered, but not as I had expected.

I would also learn an important "lesson" and "moral" that would change my life. It is this "Lesson & Moral" learned, that I will discuss a little later in this story.

As for now though some "problems" were now developing and they had to do with "jealousy." Apparently my employer began to wonder "How is "Jesse" able to afford that big Cadillac convertible? He doesn't make that kind of money here. He must have a second job. I'll have to talk to him about that."

Well it really wasn't any of his business, but he did approach me and question me about it.

"Jesse, that's quite a fine vehicle you have there. I know you said you received it as a "gift." You must have some well "heeled" friends! I was just wondering isn't that gas expensive for that vehicle? How about the insurance, it must be astronomical?"

"It is costly to operate my vehicle, but I'm able to handle it."

"Have you a 2nd job?"

"No, just working for you."

"I don't understand how you do it??"

"I get by"

Well that's pretty much what transpired with my employer. He was a "tough" individual to
work for, but I bore up with his attitude.

It seemed he never liked to see any of his employees prosper. If they did, he would complain saying, "I must be paying yall too much. You're living better than I am! I'll have to review your salaries."

And so when it came to our semi-annual time to receive our "review" for a possible pay raise, we found out those who had bought new pickup trucks, or a home, or were sporting new work clothes would cancel out any opportunity for a pay raise. He felt they were doing well, so a pay raise was not necessary.

We were upset since there were increases in taxes, gasoline prices, rentals, home prices, and our salaries were not keeping up with expences.

Some of his electricians were working side jobs, but they would never mention it to him since he would say, "I want you men to get a good nights rest so you will be able to give me a "FULL DAYS WORK." So if it was found out we had a second job, he would feel we couldn't give him our best. "You will be too tired." This was his favorite expression, and one could be immediately fired if it became known. So we kept our lips "sealed."

But for me, a "Big change" was about to Occur in my life.

A REALLY BIG CHANGE!

Chapter 17

"A dinner invitation is given"

∽೨

*I*n April of 2003 while sitting at home I received a phone call from "friend." He was his usual congenial self. I'd like you to listen into "our" conversation. It went like this...

> "Hi Jesse, how are you doing today?"
>
> "Fine "friend" and yourself?"
>
> "I'm doing OK, I called to see if you would like to have dinner with me tonight at 5:30?"
>
> "Wow that sounds great "friend!" Where do you want to meet?"
>
> "How bout us meeting at the restaurant we've been frequenting for the last few years. I know the owner and I like to contribute to his business. You know Jesse, it's *good for friends to help each other* out whenever it's possible."
>
> "Oh yes I agree 100% with you "friend" "I'll be there with "bells on my toes"...ha, ha."
>
> "Great, and maybe we can have some good old conversation about some of the "history" about Graceland, and Elvis too. How does that sound to you?"

"I'm "chomping at the bit."
"Great, see you at 5:30."

And so we met in our favorite place to eat, that
downtown *"Classy Restaurant."* This was the same restaurant where that Mother, with 4 children, after having dinner was "short" of money and couldn't pay the
bill. It also was where I met *"JB"* back in 1998 when
he had "news about Elvis" and it was here, that day,
where our "friendship" came to an end. It was also
here that "friend" and his companions overheard the
argument *"JB"* and I had over "the search" for the truth
about Elvis' death and it was then that "friend" had
quoted to me about that "Candle" in the dark filled
room. This restaurant had many "memories," many
good with "friend" and that one "Bad memory" with
"JB." Anyhow tonight would be a night with "friend"
and he always made the night enjoyable. Most of the
time we would talk about Elvis, stories about him,
places He went, people He knew, songs He sang, and
even the movies He made. "friend" was a "staunch"
"Elvis Fan." His knowledge of Elvis and of "Graceland"
was incredible!

Tonight would be a "night to remember," as I would
later find out.
"friend" was now helping me to take the "first step"
on a "New Road" that would begin a "Journey" that
would last my lifetime.
Join me and "friend" now, as we begin our dinner
together. I know you will be surprised, as I was, as the
evening comes to a close.

Chapter 18

"Decision time!"

And so I dressed up in my sporting best for dinner with "friend." It was great pulling up to that restaurant in my blue Cadillac. No walking to the downtown restaurant for this boy, I've got me a set of "wheels."

Well, when I arrived, the mater "D" saw me walk in, and immediately came over to me and welcomed me. He then said,
"Sir... please follow me... your table is waiting.

When I got there, "friend" stood up and extended his hand to me and we both shook hands. The Mater "D" then pulled out my chair for me to sit and comfortably seated me. Well, I tell you, I felt like an international dignitary. Never have I received this kind of attention. (I know he didn't see my Cadillac) Could it be because of "friend?" After all I still don't know what he does for a living, unless he's a tourist guide out at Graceland? I did see him working there as a guide not long ago.
Well who really cares? It's none of my business! Oh, here comes the waiter with some menus.

He now asks if I would like a *"cocktail,"* before Dinner. My reply...
Yes, I'll have a *"shrimp cocktail"*.....

"friend" then said to me...

"Jesse would you like an "alcoholic beverage" with your shrimp cocktail?"

"No, just a tall glass of sweet tea will do."

"friend" now orders. *"I'll have a "Martini."*
The waiter then leaves, meanwhile our Conversation now begins. *"friend"* begins the conversation.
"So tell me Jesse, how are they treating you at your place of employment?"
"Well "friend" my employer is a difficult man to work for. He expects much from all of his workers and if anyone seems to prosper he becomes jealous and reasons "maybe I'm paying them too much.... I'll have to keep that in mind when review time comes for pay raises." And sometimes we get no raise.
When he gives a raise it averages between five and ten cents an hour.
"friend" right now I am making one dollar and twenty five cents above minimum wage, and that's after working for him almost 30 years. If it were not for the "minimum wage increases" over the years God knows how much I'd be making."
"That's incredible Jesse, does he wonder how you can afford the Cadillac?"
"Oh yes we've discussed that topic shortly after you bought it for me. He has no idea you pay for my gas

and insurance. If he did I probably wouldn't have a job.

"friend," I don't understand why you do all this for me, but I assure you, I am very grateful and at night when I pray I ask God to watch over you and protect you."

"friend" seems to change the subject whenever I try to understand why He is doing all this for me? Just Listen to what He now says ...

"Jesse here comes our waiter with our drinks, are you ready to order?"
"Yes I am.
I'll have the usual, a bowl of country beans, some onion on that, some hog jawl, one pork chop and some cornbread made with some "crackle added in," and could I have a refill on that sweet tea?"

"Yes Sir"

"And You Mr. "friend?"...

"I'll have a country fried steak with gravy, some mashed potatoes, with gravy on them and some biscuits and gravy.
I'll also have a "Diet Coke" to go with my meal...
I'm trying to maintain my trim waistline, ha, ha!
("friend" has a great sense of humor, but he needs to loose a little weight, you see "friend" is a bit on the "Chunky Side"). But he is really a great friend, and that's not because he's so generous. It has to do with the "person" he is. "friend" truly *cares for people,* all people, and I really believe he is a very rare individual and someone very "special."

"Well Jesse, here comes our waiter,

74

looks like he has our meals."
The waiter then placed our meals in front
of us. Everything looked so good!

Now as we begin to "chow down," "friend"
now begins to ask me some additional questions.

"Jesse, do you have any brothers or sisters?"
No, *I am one of a set of twins. My brother was "stillborn."*

"Oh, I'm sorry to hear that Jesse. *Did your parents give him*
a name?"
**"Yes they did, it was "Elvis." Mom and dad always
said if they had twin boys they would name them "Elvis
& Jesse" after the Presley's sons.**
    **Since my brother was "stillborn," momma
decided to call him Elvis and allow me to be called
"Jesse" since I lived. She felt since Elvis Presley's
brother Jesse did not live and Elvis did,** *she would give*
"Jesse" <u>*a chance at life.*</u> **I know it sounds a bit quirky, but
"momma" was a "big" fan of Elvis.** *She loved him dearly*
as "another son." **So she felt she had both Elvis and
"Jesse" as sons,**
    while "Elvis" was still alive.

    **Maybe that sounds strange but it was how momma
felt."**

    "That's not strange at all Jesse. *It tells me much* **about
your momma's love for Elvis.**
    **I was just wondering, how would you like to quit
your job driving that truck for that electrical company,
and come work for me. I** <u>*guarantee*</u> **you will be able to
move out of that one room rental and get yourself a
nice place."**

"Gee that sounds wonderful, but where would I be working, I don't want to leave Memphis. *Memphis has been* <u>*my home*</u> all my life and I don't want to change that. I hope you understand "friend?"

"Certainly I do Jesse, and that's why I'm offering you the job. *You won't have to leave Memphis* because your *new job* is right here *in Memphis.* You see Jesse, you'll be working right here in this restaurant."

"Right here? That's great! But do you *know someone* here who will hire me?"

"I certainly do! You see Jesse *I own this* restaurant and have owned it *for many years.* Well, let's see, it was in 1971 when I purchased it from a very fine gentlemen. We knew each other for many years. In fact he offered me this restaurant at a "Steal" of a price. Of course I jumped at the "opportunity" and I purchased it. Well to be more accurate I didn't purchase it, rather let's say *we had an "understanding,"* and eventually it became mine.
He was a good man, *The people of Memphis loved him, but He passed in August of "77."*

"Boy "friend" "77" was a rough time for Memphis, Elvis, and then your friend."

"Oddly *they "<u>Both</u>" left us the very same day.*"

"The same day?" (I noticed *a tear* in "friend's" eye, as he seemed to drift off for a second.)

"friend" now quickly *changes the subject.*

"So Jesse, do you need time to make a decision?"

"No sir, count me on board!"

"Ok," then tomorrow, you show up ready for work, after you see your old employer and let him know you are leaving his employ.

We shook hands confirming the deal. A *"Hand Shake"* with *"friend"* was better than signing a contract with anyone!

His word was his guarantee and he sealed it with a *"handshake."*

At this point I had tears in my eyes and a lump in my throat. But *"friend"* wasn't finished with me yet, listen to what happened next.

"Yes Jesse, I look forward to your working at the restaurant, but first there are some necessary things we need to take care of. Come with me!"

And so we jumped into *"friend's"* Vehicle and before I knew it, *"friend"* had me in this here *"Men's Shop"* where he had me fitted with ten different suits, 15 dress shirts, twelve ties, ten pair of dress socks, and finally five pair of dress shoes. *I thought it was a bit overkill for a "dishwasher job"* so when we were driving back to the restaurant I asked *"friend"* about the new clothes.

He said, *"Jesse, what job did you think I*

was giving you?" *"Well I have no skills,"* so I thought...

"Dish washer?"

"Dish washer?"...No way! You are to be my new *"Assistant Manager,"* a position I created for YOU!

You will be working with Jerry, he's my Manager.

We served together in the *"Army"* many years ago in Germany.

"friendfromyesteryear"

I will introduce you to him *as* *"friend"* he will recognize *what that means* and you will have no problems.
"Jerry" is a *"trustworthy man."*

Chapter 19

"Adjustments....."

～

"Oh, I can't believe It, I almost forgot to tell you. Jesse, I will not have my Assistant Manager living in a "one room rental," understand?"

"Well would you feel better if I were to look for an apartment?"

"Oh no, that won't do. Tell you what I will do.

I have some rental properties of which one is a comfortable three-bedroom brick ranch. You can move in immediately. I'll give you the keys and the address so you'll be able to find the place...it might need a little "sprucing" up, and the grass may need to be cut, I'm sure you can take care of that. Oh, by the way the "residence" comes, as a benefit for being assistant manager so there will be no rental fees for you to worry about.... OK?"

(Oh my god, I couldn't believe it!)

"Well thank you again "friend" thank you, thank you, thank you!"

I just stood there in utter amazement. I felt like a king, was this really happening? Or was I just dreaming? Meanwhile I heard a voice while I was still standing there mesmerized."

"Hey Jesse... are you daydreaming? Come on you've got work to do. Take the week off to get settled in "TCB."

"By the way managers are salaried people so expect to see a paycheck this time next week when you return, and if you need a hand, just call this person."

He handed me a business card.

The name on the business card?....no name!

Just a biblical scripture. It read....proverbs 18:24b "...there exists a "friend" sticking closer than a brother"......call "a" friend at 1-***-***-****.

This was a bit much for me and so I went home to my rented one room. I sat and thought, and thought, and thought. And then I said to myself, "Why is he doing all this for me? And what is "friend's" real name?"

Now if he wanted me to know I am sure he would have told me. It would be disrespectful to ask, but I could ask him how he came to be called "friend? I think I will ask him the next time we meet, or maybe not. Oh, I'm so puzzled....

Much was yet to happen before I began to "Understand,"

"REALLY UNDERSTAND!"

The next day I headed out to my employer. I told him I was leaving. He had a real "hissy fit" and became quite vocal.

"Do you realize you won't have a steady job, Where will you go? What will you do? How will you pay your bills? You're making a big mistake Jesse. You'll come crawling back to me mark my words!"

I just thanked him for the job I had, and bid him a good day. I then told him,

"I'm sure we'll see each other again."

That night I spoke to my landlord, *"Miss Diane,"* and she was very sad over the news that I would be leaving before the end of the month. I still recall her words, such a sweet old lady.

Jesse, I have known you for some 20 years or more. Are you not happy living here? If there is something I can do to make you happy just tell me, please. *I don't want to see you leave."*

"Miss Diane, I want to thank you for your hospital-ity all these years, I have been "happy living here" and you have treated me like a son, I thank you.

In life we make decisions and those decisions we make *have consequences,* some are bad and some are good. I truly believe the decision I have made is a good one that will eventually bear good fruitage.

This *"decision"* requires me to leave one *"life style behind"* to start a *"new life."* Miss Diane I'm not getting any younger. I need to act on my decision. I need to do it *"my way."* So please try to understand. The

... "time" has come."

"I understand Jesse and although I will miss you, I'll know you will be happy, and that makes me happy too."

The next morning I drove out to the house that *"friend"* was allowing me to live in. When I arrived at the address I stopped my car, and just marveled at what I saw. I checked my notes to make sure I was at the right place, and I sure was.

The home sat on about 4 acres of Beautiful professionally manicured lawn and shrubbery.

Beautiful fruit trees, apples, pears, and pecans. Also "flowering" pinks and white dogwoods. So many others I couldn't even begin to name or number.

I then drove up the driveway, parked my Caddy and stepped out onto the driveway. I now walked up to the house and as I stepped up to the door and started to use my house key the door suddenly opened. There stood a young woman dressed nicely but apparently she was a domestic.

She then introduced herself to me and said, "friend" said you would be here soon and we were to get everything in order. If you find you need something just use the number you were given on that business card. We'll take care of the rest. Ok?"

So I asked her where the lawnmower was so I could cut the grass when it came time.

She smiled and said, "You won't be cutting grass, you're "friend's" assistant manager. We care totally for this Estate. While you're out we will see that you're rooms are cleaned daily, beds made, and *if you need anything from the "Market," foods, snacks, any beverages, in short we are here to care for your needs.* We hope you will be happy living here."

Well I tell you I couldn't believe my ears, and this place was a virtual "paradise."

All for me...why? I would one day, very soon, find out.

Chapter 20

"The End of the Beginning"

⟿

Now in this "Fictional" Story we have found many "similaritys between Elvis and Jesse." They both came from "Humble" beginnings, both had life changing experiences, neither could believe what was happening in their lives would "Last," for it all seemed like a "fairytale" existance. Both made life changing decisions for "Jesse" things seemed to turn out well....for Elvis things turned out differently.

"friend" now recalls to me what was said as they met at Graceland on that fateful day. Let's return one "last" time to August 16, 1977.

"friend" begins to speak...
"It was evening of the 16th of August. Yes, The world had been informed of the passing of "The King." Those of us who were "left"
now gathered at "Graceland" for instruction.

"It seems just like "yesterday," and yet in my mind's eye I clearly recall these words....

⟳

"So what's next?"...a familiar voice now replies, "well..." he pauses....he appears extremely nervous,
    his face pales with anxiety and as he replies
    his voice begins to crack......
    tears are falling from his eyes,
    "all is going according to plan. You all know how serious those 'death threats' had been & certainly HE had no freedom to move around as you all do. He's been a 'prisoner' of his fame, tired, sick,
    lonely & extremely sad. At least now He has peace.
    He will be more famous in "Death" than in life,
    as sad as that may be. I know perhaps that some may feel I'm being callused, but you all know that He would want us to try to look at the "bright side" and not focus on the negative.

"I know yall concerned and that's why I've gathered "You," you who are the ones left, of whom Elvis considered his remaining friends, "The inner Circle." You know the rest have abandoned him, a couple have even written a so called "Tell All" book that has hurt Elvis greatly, it's unbelievable what some will do for "money." They even claimed they were trying to "help" Him by writing their "book."

I then spoke ("friend")

"Just one point... Please"... As I asked permission to speak."

84

What are we to say to all the Fan clubs that are already ringing the phones off the hook

...Oh God!... What will we say?

"I've taken care of that and my instructions are all "Fan Clubs" on the official registry are to be contacted & those instructions are being carried out at this very moment."

"What are they being told to do, after all they'll be clamoring to be here out of respect for Him."

"Zion, please pass me my clipboard. Let me see my notes. Let's see now.... Our "intimate" Public Relations people are to be informed to communicate to all Fan Clubs listed on our official registry. They are to be told to try and understand why we cannot accommodate their wishes and delay this process. There is utter chaos here. Memphis is overrun with grief. People are passing out all over the place, some have gone into shock, others have been hospitalized and there is even greater sadness in that we've received word of at least 2 fatalities having to do with individuals being hit by vehicles...

Men, we want to get this thing over as fast as possible. The longer we prolong this, the greater the chance there will be other tragedies. We certainly don't want to have that happen. We all know what our responsibilities are at this point. If anyone is not 100% sure as to what his or her role is at this time, then please speak up now.... OK?"

Now As "friend" continues to relate those events....he now reveals additional information for us....

"Now the room took on a different atmosphere,
some of us were just sitting, hands were clasped
over our faces...we were crying.... We couldn't believe
that Elvis, truly had...."Left the Building."

It was then that I was told why the name "friend"
was given to me. While we were meeting together
that evening as instructions were being given I was
questioned:

"By the way "friend"..... Has Elvis ever said why
He calls you "friend"?
"No sir.... He just used that expression whenever
referring to me.... I couldn't care what He called me. I
was just happy being part of the "family."
"Well it is quite obvious Elvis had great affection
for you. You're the youngest member of "The Inner
Circle," and so I tell you this "friend"....
When Elvis used the term "friend" he was pay-
ing you a Great Honor. You see Elvis knew well in
advance that one day, this would all end. The fairytale
would come to its last page and then one would have
no choice but to "close the book."
He also knew that after his "death" there would
come individuals who would try to discredit him, paint
him in a bad light, tell vicious lies, even say cruel
things about his Family...
He realized there would be great "speculation"
on "how" and "why" he died, by "natural causes or
evil means." He knew there would be those who
would "capitalize" on His "demise." Then of course
the "Books" would come "explaining" it all. None
would
have it correct and none would have the
"Presley families" blessing...

Therefore in "Defense" of Elvis, since He could no longer defend himself, there would "rise" those who would do all "they" could, to protect the "Elvis Legacy" & the "Family Name."

These He would consider His "TRUE FRIENDS" and His extended family... even in death, and so the expression, "friend" which in "his" mind, was equated with those who were, and would, become "Loyal Friends."

This does not mean the rest of the remaining "circle" would not be considered "friend"....

He used "you" to stand out as different among others by calling you "friend." You are the youngest and you represent all those who will come along, some not even born as of this day and *"They" would "Defend" the "Legend" and*

The "Family Name" seeing to it that the "Truth" would always be told. You "friend" are the first of a new generation of "friends."

Whether the threats would come from newspapers, TV talking points, verbal, or any other forms of abuse there may be or yet come to be, they would care for it.

To these Elvis referred to as "friend." Although they are "individuals" from all walks of life as a "group" they would be classed as a "family of friends."

One day, you "friend" will find the "one" who will write The Book that will explain what happened here on this mournful day.

That person, "after your demise," will write the book. It will be called "The Final Curtain, a Love Story Untold." It can be "Released" on the first day of the month of August 2014, or in time for the "night" of the candle light vigil on August 15, basically any time between 8/15 and January 8th 2015, when Elvis would have been 80 years of age, had He lived. Reason being, *there will probably be much grief in Memphis during those occasions.*

When the "Book" is read, it will bring peace and a sense of "closure." It won't answer everything, that will require more "Time." But it will give them enough "Light" to understand the "Greater Picture," just like "One Candle" burning in a Darkened Room," and those who have made wild claims will have their "Mouths" silenced.

They will then understand why "The Book" was published. Yes the "friends" will get "The Message."

"friend" speaks again,

"The last words I heard as we all exited Graceland that day were these."

"But for now "friends"... We've got work to do... come on boys, you too "friend"...

LET'S T.C.B. !.... Zion, please.... turn off all the "lights" when you "lock up" the place,...thanks Zion"

ᶜ⌒ᴐ

And now "friend" concludes his words with tears in his eyes saying...

"And so went the meeting that mournful day, 8/16/77"

Yes, I came to understand why I had been called "friend" and I have kept that as my "secret" until now.

As for me, "there's not much time left." That's why I've been "grooming" you for your next assignment. When I pass from this world you will become "friend" in fact I have considered you as "friend" for quite some time now. Ever since you made your stand against "JB,"...... "WE" knew "You" were next in line to be part of the "Inner Circle." We're always searching, searching, searching.

We knew earlier that you could only afford that "rented one room" and that you could have made much money publishing a book that would "Tickle the Ears of Many."

But your action that day "confirmed" your "love and respect" for Elvis and his family, especially when you mentioned Elvis little "sweetheart" Lisa Marie, and how opening a can of worms would serve no purpose except to

rehash things that can only cause more suffering on the family. A family that gave it ALL....even Her "father's "Life" to His fans.

You showed us you were a curious individual. Your curiosity was nothing more than what millions of other "honest hearted" fans may have wondered and hoped could be that Elvis "faked" his death, and was still with us.

Sadly that's not true.

We knew for years how much you supported the annual Elvis Celebrations. At times we Worried that your economic situation might move you to seek out employment in another area and not in Memphis Tennessee. You see it is "here" that "things happen."

The "spirit" of Elvis permeates this entire Globe. So individuals are constantly hearing Elvis songs, dancing to His music, and wishing... "If only He had lived..."

Now Jesse asks some "questions" so he will be adequately prepared with answers to "questions" that many believe indicate that Elvis did not die but rather "Faked his death."

Some of these Points seem to indicate Elvis is still alive.

∽◯

"friend" there are "questions" many have about Elvis' death, some I believe out of shear "curiosity," others to be trouble makers, and of course there are others who out of "Sincere Love" would hope Elvis made his "Great Escape" and has enjoyed a new life of "Peace & Happiness."

May I have the "Honor" of asking you 5 questions that pertain to what I've just stated so that I may be adequately qualified to defend the "Truth?"

"Jesse go right ahead and ask..."

• "friend" Was Elvis planing to leave the entertainment business?

"Well Jesse, Elvis always wanted to have a "family." He wanted more children, and he wanted to be "happily" married." He never really got over the breakup of His marriage to Priscilla. He loved her till his dying day. The marriage just couldn't be "reconciled." It would not be proper for me say anything more since it would be my opinion and that would not be fair to state as "fact."

"friend" now leans forward in his "easy" chair, points his index finger towards me and now as he's "shaking that finger" tells me... "I tell you this, "IF," Elvis wanted to leave it all "behind and start a new life," IT COULD HAVE BEEN ACCOMPLISHED! Elvis had the "Money," the "Connections" with high level government officials & the "Determination." He had everything to pull it off!

But Now,.... "friend" falls back into his "easy chair" and a "tear" falls from his eye...He then looks me straight in the eyes and says very solemnly ... "Yes Elvis had it "All"...but sadly He ran out of what he needed most of all, and neither "Money" nor "Influence" could help....

"Our "Friend" ran out of ...Time..."

"friend" was noticeably saddened so we took a coffee break, he talked about "Life" and how "precious" life is.
"friend" now focuses on how important it is to use our lives properly.
"Jesse count your days wisely," for tomorrow is promised to no one." YES, Life is one "Short ride down a Long and often bumpy road"...So Carefully choose "The One" to Ride with you "Lovingly" for "She" wll be your "Ticket to happiness. As Elvis knew right to the "end," there can only be "One True Love," one "Ticket," and for "Him" it was always "Priscilla" right down to his dying day ..." YES, Hold Her Tightly, give Her the "Love" and attention she will always desire, make "Her" your one love in life for as the "conductor" says,... "One Ticket (True Love) per person," ....
So hold onto "Her"
tightly, yes "Love & Life" are Gifts", ever so "fragile" not to be squandered and given so Generously by our

"Creator." ....(Psalm: 36:9)

So let's not put off the ... "I Love You"...till
tomorrow, for "Tomorrow" is always one day away
and "The Ride"... Will Always be Shorter Than You
Think....We "finish" our days in a *Whisper."*

❧

Yes "friend" was a very "wise" man. I know he did
sit in on those "Bible study groups" with Elvis on
many occasions. I guess that was where he gained the
"Wisdom" of life as he explained it to me.

It looks like he's ready to answer more questions.
Let's see.

❧

"friend" now sits back in that nice and comfy easy
chair and resumes answering my first question.

Yes Jesse, sadly "death" would overtake Elvis before
he could make "His Great Escape."

Interestingly his "77" concert series had what "many
believe" were "Cryptic messages," given out in a number of song choices Elvis made.

Let me give you a few examples:

When he sang "If you love me let me know, if you
don't then let me go,...... take these chains away that
keep me loving you."(some ask the question) "Who
was he singing to?"

When he sang "are you lonesome tonight?" (Some
ask, Why did he say "I know only 3 chords, I fooled
many for a "long time.") Then at the end of the song

he stated, *"...if you don't come back, then "They can bring the Final Curtain down."*

Of course when he sang "My way," that really opened the door for individuals to read into it what they hoped or honestly thought was true.

(They felt he was telling us he was going to "pack it in,"...the "final curtain"... "do it my way"...etc.).... or so they said.

One other point they claim indicated he was preparing to "Make His Great Escape" and start a new life, had to do with the same song, "My Way." Some feel Elvis "faked" not knowing the words to "My Way," to bring "special emphasis" on the "Words" of that song. He then started to read the words from a sheet of paper...and shortly into the song he never looked down at the paper again...could his declining health and use of medication been the reason? Only God knows.

Elvis "definitely" knew the words, since He sang "My Way" on numerous occasions. People can read into it whatever they want to. The bottom line is this, if Elvis wanted to leave it all behind he sadly ran out of his most precious commodity... "Time."...Think about that!

2. "friend" there have been many who have stated "Elvis filled out his own death certificate." How am I to understand the truth about that?"

"Oh that's an easy one to explain. You see Jesse, Elvis loved to play tricks on his friends. On one occasion Elvis decided to fake his death to see the reaction of his friends. He allowed one friend who was in on the prank to "shoot him" with a pistol loaded with blanks. He then fell down "dead," and a blood patch used in acting was actuated to make it appear he was truly shot. As he lay there he would "listen" to the "friends" REACTIONS, and finally jump up revealing the "hoax."

Elvise also presented a death certificate completely filled out and signed. He listed his bodyweight I believe to be 165 lbs. At Elvis' death he weighed a little more than 200 pounds. Anyone with "conspiracy" thoughts should have realized the death certificate they found, or bought from someone, who may have kept the certificate to one day start the "Mystique" around Elvis' death, had to be a false certificate. There's much money out there to be made on a falsity when evil ones try to tamper with so called "Evidence." But it's so easily "seen" why the so called "Death Certificate" is a false document. Understand Jesse?

"Yes I do "friend."....

3.   "Thank you." Now here's another. Why is Elvis name misspelled on his Grave Marker?

"Ah ha. The truth of the matter is also very simple. When Elvis was born, his mother Gladys named him Elvis "Aaron" Presley. Vernon was worried since Gladys was of Jewish decent that in the south "Jewish people" might be harassed. So he had her keep her "ancestry private." He also had Elvis middle name Aaron changed to Aron.

In biblical history in the "Hebrew Aramaic" scriptures commonly referred to as "The Old Testament," the Jewish "Priestly class" were all taken from the Aaronic lineage. "Aaron" being Israel's "1st high priest." So it's believed by many Vernon wanted to "protect" his son from possible harassment. So the name on the birth certificate was changed to Aron.

Elvis grew up with that name knowing what his father had done to protect Gladys and his son, Elvis.

So Elvis signed all his papers, Elvis aron Presley. Army papers, Elementary & high school registration, marriage license. *His career saw him as Elvis "Aron" Presley. (THE "IMAGE" PLAYED OUT IN LIFE.....his "Role" in Life.)*

I also believe the colonel was worried people would find out Elvis' mother was Jewish and "that knowledge" might effect Elvis' career.

Elvis, on the other hand, was more concerned about his mother than his career, and would not do anything to bring any shame on her, whether or not people in the South liked or disliked Jewish people. Elvis loved his mother dearly.

Elvis did eventually realize his health was on a decline. He wanted to honor his mother even in "Death." He tried to do so in life when he bought her "Graceland" and a pink Cadillac, but she passed away shortly thereafter. *So it was in "Death" he wished to be remembered <u>by the name</u> he was so "Honorably given" by his mother, "Elvis Aaron Presley," in essence <u>"Stepping Out" of "The Image"</u> ... <u>"Elvis "aron" Presley" and being "Remembered" as .. "Elvis Aaron Presley."</u> (Try reading this again, remember Elvis also admitted while alive that we all play many "Roles" in LIFE. He also stated there is a difference between "THE MAN & THE IMAGE" And then emphasized it's VERY HARD TO LIVE UP TO AN IMAGE.)*

He also felt this would show "respect" for his mother's "Jewish ancestry." *Never forget, and <u>this is "CLUE" to ALL the so called "Mystique" surrounding the "death" of Elvis.</u> If He would have "faked" His death He NEVER would have "Dishonored" the "Name given by his Mother at birth by falsely having it inscribed on his grave marker, especially since He KNEW what it meant to her. <u>Elvis was superstitious yes, but He would Never "Play" with the Name of "Israel's 1st High Priest "Aaron." Elvis knew His Bible and had great respect for "The Word."</u>*

This analogy is in direct contrast to what others have said, wherein they claim "He faked His death" and due to "superstition" He "feared" tempting "Fate" and so had his name intentionally mispelled on his Grave Marker."

As one can now see, to use His "changed at birth name" associated with "THE IMAGE," Knowing at "Death" the image would also die, would be inconsistant with His wish which was to be buried and "Remembered" with the Original name given to him by his Mother Gladys. (Elvis "Aaron" Presley).

If His "Death" was "Faked," then to Inscribe the Original Name given at birth "Elvis "Aaron" Presley falsely on His grave marker would be seen as <u>inconsistant</u> with His love for His Creator, His Mother, and respect for the Word of God. The "FACT" that it IS inscribed STRONGLY INDICATES He Truly is buried at "Graceland."(I know it's a bit confusing but read it again and again if necessary.)

❧

Now Elvis had but "4" real "loves" in His life. His "Creator," His "Mother," His "Wife," and lastly but certainly not "least" His beautiful little daughter "Lisa Marie." Any others, although he may have loved these as "friends" none ever, really took the place of **"Priscilla."**

"That's so beautiful "friend." So please, just two more questions."

4. There was speculation that the corpse on display for viewing was not Elvis, supposedly even a cousin and some Fans agreed it did not look like Elvis. They "saw" what appeared as beads of sweat on his forehead, and one sideburn was supposedly "lifted" off his face, as if it were glued on.

Is there anything I can say about that, and did "You see Elvis" in the casket at viewing time when those "Special Guests" were invited to the "Memorial Services?"

"friend" now replies in a bit of anguish.

"I'll say this, it's no bodies BUSINESS How the family handled the Memorial, the Viewing, and the Burial! That was "their grief" and although we too were grieved, none of us could feel the pain they all suffered. Never forget that!

Maybe an illustration might suffice for you Jesse. Tell me, if you had a son, who was loved by millions, even to the point of idolizing him, and now he has suddenly died, and thousands upon thousands of fans appear in Memphis, knowing how fans in the past tore his

Antennae off his car, mirrors off his car, license plate off his car, all in an attempt to get a "souvenir," do you think you might be concerned about your son's body being desecrated unknowingly by fans "crazed" in their grief, "blinded" like a mob out of control because of their "love" for this man? Embracing, tugging, pulling at the corpse out of "excruciating pain of heart." These fans loved him so much. Many might lose control of themselves and thus desecrate the corpse.

Would "you" put the body of "your son" out for display with such a very real chance of things getting terribly out of control?

Tell me, if they would have put him in a "Gated" crypt, what "GATE" could hold such a mass of humanity from "Ripping the Gate right off it's hinges?"

Wouldn't it be better to put a "Decoy" figure and dress it as best to resemble "Elvis" and keep the "real corpse" in a hidden place protected at Graceland **until Vernon could get the necessary permits to bury Elvis there.** *A "faked attempt" to steal the "fake Elvis" from the Gated Crypt would "ensure" and set all the "ducks in a row" so that the "Real Elvis" could be buried at Graceland."*

And so, There He "rests," at home at Graceland."

Now your last question *if I saw "Elvis" in the casket…***I will tell you about that at a later time…***now is "not" the time to answer that question…Ok?*

Sure "friend," and again I "sincerely thank you." One final question please.

5. Why is Elvis not buried where he said he wanted to be, next to his mother, instead of being buried between His Father and Grandmother?

I Remind you once again, "Remember this," ** *The "Key" to understanding the entire "Story" hangs on the "Spelling" of his "NAME" on His grave marker,* **and the outstanding *"Love"* **and "Respect" He had for** *His "Mother." His* **"knowledge & respect" for** *God's word, "The Bible." As far as "Any" other so called "evidence" raised by Anyone, whether Elvis Immatator," numerology, no flaged draped Coffin, Doctors, lawyers, medical examiners or people who claim to have a "special" relationship with Elvis, they ALL ARE "TRUMPED" by THE "SPELLING" of The Name "Elvis Aaron Presley" on the grave marker for the reasons stated above.*

Yes, one would be able to understand why he is "where" he is from those points alone. But if an individual is not "Spiritually inclined," it then becomes almost impossible to "understand." *It's that simple.*

Remember Elvis was a very "Humble" & religious man. He knew one day He would be *"reunited" with His Mother* **again,** *by means of a "resurrection" from the dead. (John 5:28&29)* **so in His mind showing "Honor, Respect, Humility, and "Love" for His Creator and His Mother in "This life" would "Assure" Him of "seeing" Her again when they eventually would be "Reunited."**

Elvis was a very "Deep Thinking," and "Spiritually Complex" man.

I'll explain this in a little greater detail.

In the "Jewish Household" the "Man" is considered "The Head," of the family. *To usurp that "headship" would be a "dishonor." So in recognition of his "Mothers" Jewish heritage Elvis would not want to dishonor her by usurping his Father's "headship,"* doing so *by insisting* on being buried next to his mother, *the location being properly "Theocratically" assigned to the "father."*
So Elvis is where He is, buried between his father and his grandmother, the "Father" being next to Gladys, his "wife" when she was alive. *Indeed Elvis was a* <u>Humble man</u> *and a true believer in the* <u>"Bible"</u> *as the* **"FINAL AUTHORITY"** <u>He chose it to be his "Final Authority" both in life & when he realized He was facing "The Final Curtain...Death."</u>

It's best for us to accept the "Truth," and learn from the decisions Elvis made. He was bigger than life and yet is no longer with us in the flesh. The "memories" the "music" the "movies," will Never be forgotten and the story of, "The poor boy from Tupelo who was allowed to live a "fairytale life," will be told from generation to generation for as long as this "Old world" continues on.

Yes Elvis was able to do for others what He could not do for himself, find "True happiness, love, generosity, and compassion in a "family" setting.
He gave these things unselfishly to all but in return received disappointment from so called close friends.
One of Elvis' religious beliefs as stated by Jesus at Mathew 7:12 said, "Do unto others what you would like others to do unto you," it's known as *"The Golden Rule."* In following that teaching, Elvis would Still experience, the "Joy that filled His Heart," as he would "See" the happiness he could impart to a

"LIVE" audience, through his music, love, and generosity to many who knew him, and even poor souls "HE" never "knew," as these would benefit from this man's amazing generosity. His *"Love for others"* **and living by His religious beliefs was the "Motivating force" in His life, it was what "sustained" him in his last days.** *It was by the "Grace of God," That He was given the "Strength" to finish his "77" concert series.*

"So,"... *do you see Jesse, why it is* **so important** *for the "Entire"* *"77" Final Concert Series to be released?"* **It will show what is really important to see, and that is this. Here was a man who by the "Grace of God," was allowed to live long enough to** *"make a "Statement." That statement was this. "One can only get from life what one "Generously Gives" to Others." So we need to exert ourselves. Elvis "Gave" to all of "US" what he never "Received" from many of his ... "So called" ... "friends," ...*

<u>*"Elvis gave us His Heart"... "broken"*</u>
...and...

<u>**"Dying."**</u>

They just ate, and ate.

Consuming "Him" piece by piece.

But *"The Blessing Elvis received from "us," His fans, was "Love" ...* *"Never Ending Love."...* **Enormously"** *...from His* **"Fans!"**
Because of his giving so generously and I'm not speaking of money, or material gifts, *I'm speaking about Elvis "giving His Heart to us."* **He in turn received untold blessings.** *The "Greatest Blessing" Elvis received, was that of a good Relationship with His Creator, the second in my humble opinion was and continues to be the "Family" he always wanted, and that filial (Family) came from the <u>"Millions</u>*

of Fans" from all over the World. And that "Family" from all races, colors, national origins, continues to "Love Him" even 35 plus years since His passing.

To me it's nothing short of **"Miraculous."**

Yes, God Indeed Blessed the "poor boy" from tupelo, and none of us will ever forget him....

Jesse there is always a "reason" why things turn out as they do in life.

Today people want to know why, how, is it really true? *I ask, "Is it our "Business" to question "Why?"* Do we really need to know "how," and if we are told He has died, should we not be "Satisfied" with that for an answer and not try to "perpetuate a lie" giving false hopes to those so very vulnerable, the fans, in a effort to enrich ourselves at their expense and then there's the "Heartache" one brings on The Presley family by perpetuating a "Myth", or a an outright lie?

Jesse never let yourself forget those words I spoke to you long, long, long ago....

"Does not one candle in a room full of darkness make a bright light?"

"Too much light can be blinding."

"Thank you "friend," I understand perfectly. It makes perfect sense, and I appreciate your explaining it so carefully for me."

"friend" speaks again:

I knew you would understand why He is where He is, with just a little help, and that makes me so happy, because it has really "confirmed in my mind" *that "You" are "Truly the one we have searched for" to carry on the "Work."*

"friend" continues to speak:

Yes Jesse we know "The Truth." Very few will be able to discern that. Elvis left us many, many, years ago. But He NEVER left us "entirely."

A "New Generation" *is being raised with his music. His music is "Timeless" and why is this so? Because Elvis gave us songs of "Love," songs to laugh with, cry with, dance to.*

His Gospel singing was "unequaled" as many would say, and why? Because what he sang about He truley "believed"…

We have his movies, we have his music, and we have "Graceland."

We have Priscilla and "Lisa Marie" who have done wonders with Graceland, helping "tirelessly" to keep the "fairytale" ALIVE! And they have been faithful to that endeavor.

But Sadly Jesse, most of those who were with me that day are no longer alive. We have all grown old. But you are still somewhat young, and will probably live many more years. I pray that your life will be long, filled with many opportunities to do good for people."

"Jesse" now replies with tears in his eyes,

"friend," "I understand."

"friend" now speaks concerning what Elvis' name has done for "Memphis" since that sad day.

"Yes Jesse, since Elvis' passing, there have been enormous sales of records, albums, movies, CD's, DVD's anything "Elvis."

There are fans all over the world that have collected all types of Elvis Memorabilia. Some of these collections are worth fortunes.

Memphis has become a "Magnet" for fans "The World Over."
The Annual Elvis "candle light vigils", Christmas at Graceland, Birthday celebrations, Elvis week at Memphis, and the list goes on and on.

Graceland has become the 2nd most visited place in the U.S. next to "The White House," in Washington D.C."

Now it's true Elvis did not want "Memphis" to ever be forgotten, mind you NOT that He was looking for any "glory" due to the "name" he made for himself, but rather Memphis was not to be forgotten financially.
He cared for everyone, and so in memory of Elvis "We" have done everything out of respect for His "name" and as a consequence of showing "respect," His fans throughout the world have responded "immensely" by keeping the "Memory" alive. This in turn has provided a
"Blessing" not only for the "Merchants" in Memphis, but for "Millions around the world."
Think of all the "Elvis" impersonators all over the world who are able to make a good "living" for themselves and their families by imitating Elvis. The sellers of DVD's and CD's, movies, memorabilia and the list go on infinitum.
There is no "economic stimulus plan" that can come close to what Elvis, one man, has done to create jobs for millions, even after having passed away more than 35 years ago.

This does not take into consideration the various "Charities Around The World" that "Elvis Presley Enterprises" and "Graceland," with the help of "Priscilla" & "Elvis" little sweetheart "Lisa Marie," have supported with financial aide. It was said that "Elvis" supported some fifty Charities in "Memphis" alone.

One place I will never forget is "Saint Jude's Children's Hospital," in Memphis. That Hospital is dedicated to finding a cure for childhood cancers and they have come a long way in preserving the young lives of these unfortunate but "Well loved" children.

Saint Jude's was the "lifelong work" of singer & entertainer Danny Thomas. Without him and his daughter, Marlo Thomas, another "Sweetheart" who continues to help since the "passing" of her father, That Hospital, would not exist today. It has an outstanding "Policy" of "No child is ever turned away from life saving medical care due to inability to pay."

So even in "death" Elvis continues to support millions.

Jesse, "We" want the "good family name" of "Presley" not tarnished in any way. Elvis was a man of "extraordinary talent," He "cared for people." He never forgot His "roots" and as unbelievable as it might sound, Elvis never realized how "famous," he truly was.

Yes, He indeed was a "humble man."

And so Jesse, in the course of "time," "Graceland" became a tourist attraction that 'Every Elvis Fan' from all over the world would try to visit at least once in their lives.

Yes the "HOME" of a man who lived
a "Fairytale life".

But, "This fairytale," as in all "fairytales," does
indeed have a "happy ending"... The "Memory and
Music" lingers on.

For generation after generation, the story will be told of poor "country folks," and how their son rose to become one of the greatest entertainers of all time, and in the "eyes" of millions, "The "Greatest."

Yes God blessed the "Poor boy from Tupelo," he left us riches that we never knew existed. A "tremendous love for his God, his Family, and humanity."

(Just listen to Elvis sing ... "If I Can Dream.")..before concluding this Book. Yes take a minute to listen to that recording.

This He so often expressed beautifully in song.
Songs such as "How Great Thou Art," Take my hand
precious lord," "Don't Cry Daddy," In The Ghetto,"
"The Wonder of You," "Can't Help Falling in Love With
You" and "If I Can Dream."
I'd better stop here since the list goes on and on.
What more can I say Jesse?
We know what we "need to know." We need nothing else, for if we have not been told anything more about His "passing" then there's nothing more for "us" to know, or it's simply not our business, or not true. Leave it at that.
If anything needs to be "told" the Presley family, at
their discretion, will share it with us.

Remember Jesse what I told you many years ago...?

"Does not one "candle" in a room full of darkness make a bright "light?"

"friendfromyesteryear"

"Too much "light" can be Blinding!

And so our *"Elvis"* has gone to *"rest."* But THAT *"Candle"* continues to ...

"BURN BRIGHTLY!"

∽

Chapter 21

"The loss of a "friend"

~

"friend" and I shared one last candlelight vigil that year. The night happened to be a bit "breezy."
Interestingly while "friend" and I were standing together with our candles, a boy about 16 years of age came to be standing alongside us. His candle kept "blowing out" and I could see he was getting "teary eyed." I looked at "friend" and "friend" nodded his head with a big smile. So I said to the young man,

"Having a tough time keeping your candle lit on this "breezy" evening I see."

"Yes," he replied, "and *I have no more matches.*"

"Well that's no problem young man, here, hold your candle next to mine and I'll give you a light." With that my candle lit his candle, he smiled, I brushed away the tear from his eye, and He thanked me.

He then said "my candle doesn't make a whole lot of Light" but all of us "together," are sure "Lighting up this place!" I smiled and said:

"Yes, *"together" we can make a big difference can't we?"* ...
"YES SIR!!"

I turned and "friend" was smiling from one ear to the other. I whispered to "friend,

"I think this is going to be the "beginning" of a "loooong... friendship!"

The three of us struck up a friendship that night. That summer Anthony came to work for us at the restaurant. We affectionately called him "Tony." He had moved to Memphis from Long Island New York, and would finish school that summer. So we added a new "member" to our "family."

Tony would grow to be a fine young man who cared "unselfishly" for others. Just the kind of man we would need.

That summer while Tony was cleaning off tables an argument erupted. Some big man was screaming at Tony. Tony was speaking nicely to the man but the man wouldn't stop. I decided see what was going on. Who was this noisy customer? You'll never guess!

"He" looked at me and said, "what are you doing here?"
"Waiting on tables?"
It was
My "Old Boss"
from the electrical company!
I then told him, "Sorry to Disappoint you but I'm The Manager!
He kept a fussing and so I had him removed from the restaurant by the Memphis Police.

(I love those boys!)
They wanted to know if I wanted to press charges of disorderly conduct. My old boss's complexion changed and also his attitude. I told the police if he promises not to cause any more
Problems "I'll let him go." I could see he was fuming. But he promised and so I let him go.

Ya know, it kinda felt "Good" fixing his old wagon! It was long overdue for all he did and probably continued to do to his employees..

But as Elvis once said as he quoted from the "Bible" ...

"Whatever a man sows, so shall he reap."

Yep, Elvis also once said, *"I hope you get what you want in life, but I'm "SURE" you'll "Always" get what you "DESERVE!"......I* don't think that was from the "BIBLE"...maybe???? at least that's what "friend" told me He said.

⟳

"friend" would tell me of times he spent with Elvis and apparently Elvis had many sayings he would quote from the "Bible."
Elvis taught them much.
At times he would hold a little "Bible discussion." They would listen and at times make comments. Everyone had the opportunity to express their opinion, **but** *Elvis would always lean on "The Word" as the*
"final authority."
Those Sessions
coupled with some gospel songs made for an enjoy-able evening. ❋❋❋
❋❋❋❋❋❋

As time would have it life continued to move on. I had learned much from "friend" and Jerry. Kindness, unselfishness, compassion, trust, loyalty and most of all I learned how to "Love."
"Time" was moving on....and my life was heading for a big change. In January of 2012, I met the woman I would shortly marry, a "Nurse," while visiting a Friend

at the "Veteran's hospital" in Nashville. Her name was "Peggy Sue" but she preferred "Patches." She told me she was called 'Patches' because She had been in the military (Army), some years back and served as a "medic." The "boys" called Her "Patches" because she would "tend to their medical needs while in combat. She had been married but "lost her husband of 19 years while in combat. Now "Patches" was a bit younger than me but we were in "Love" and that's all that was "necessary" and so "Patches" and I were married 4 months after we met on April 21, 2012. "friend" was my "Best man" on that "beautiful" day. After the wedding "friend" surprised us with a "Reception" at His Restaurant. "friend" had The Place "Decorated" absolutely "beautiful." He also called in some "boys" He knew from "Nashville" to play for the gathering. (a "Blue Grass" band.) Patches & I danced our first "dance" to "Never Ending Love," by ...oh you know... of course "The King of R&R.....our dear friend ELVIS!

And then We went "All out" with that "Blue Grass." Well i'll be a tellen ya, We had us a "BIG TIME."

The next day my Legs were a killen me. And "Patches" did what she knew needed to be done, she gave my legs "massage therapy" she has a wonderful "woman's touch, so I decided I would "heal" nice and slow, real "slooooooooow." She said it would take a couple of days until I would be well mended........ so I followed her diretions, "yes indeedy" nice and "Slooooooooow."

As time moved on, I found myself recalling the words of an old song from long, long ago entitled, "Into each life some rain must fall." And with all the good that was happening in our lives, "rain" would begin to fall, and fall it did when "friend" was hospitalized.

Sadly one week after "friend" was admitted to the hospital he "peacefully passed away." Patches, Tony and I were by His side. He spoke one last time, but before He spoke He asked "Patches" & Tony to leave The room. He wanted this to be a "Private Moment" between the two of us. And so He began...

You know Jesse, you have become a "son" to me. I love you very much. As you know I never married and so I have no children. You have filled that "void" in my life. Thank you my "son." In life we all make decisions.

Those "Decisions" have "consequences," for me, for you, & for Elvis. As you know, Elvis was a DEA man. As such he had very real threats against his life, and his family was also in danger. This brought Him great stress. There were individuals who wanted Elvis "dead" for his work in the DEA. (Drug Enforcement Agency) Elvis did much to help the country rid itself of a number of "Drug Lords." But there are "consequences" to the decisions we make in life.

His decision to help in the area of "Drug Enforcement" brought with it real dangers. These too would bring additional "stress" to His life.

Eventually one day he would die as we all eventually do Jesse, but sadly in his case he would "die young." Elvis had many life threatening health issues. These issues "controlled his "Decisions" to Use the prescription medications he needed to "continue on."

He was a "slowly dying man" for a long time. It didn't happen overnight, but the consequences of "Death Threats," "Failed Marriage," His love for His little "sweetheart" Lisa Marie and concerns for her and her momma's safety, coupled with a "Crushing work load," at times 3 concerts a night, and of course "Parker" who pushed him to the "Breaking Point," all led to "August 16, 1977."

Despite all the health issues and astronomical "Stress" He was under, it would still come as a "shock" to the "World" when we all heard all over the World, on T.V. or the radio the sad news that:

"Elvis Presley"
the "King of Rock & Roll" has died.

We were indeed saddened, and "Shocked.".

But even more sadness would come, as critics would state unkind things about Elvis.
Such accusations as, "He was a Drug Addict."
That would be the saddest I felt, since Elvis "Risked His life" to help "His Country" rid itself of Drug traffickers, Drug Lords etc. These accusations were baseless.
On the other hand, Some would say Elvis "abused" the prescription medications He needed.

Tell me Jesse, have you ever taken A number of prescription medications you had to take that would perhaps make you a little confused or drowsy? Is it possible you could have "accidentally overdosed" on one or more prescription medications? Is it possible "THAT" was the situation with Elvis? And could this continue to happen more and more frequently as His health progressively declined?

Yes Jesse always look "Beyond what may seem Obvious, because *"Truth"* does not find it's place with the majority, it's *"only revealed"* to those whose "Hearts" are righteously disposed to *"Love."* Always look for the "Good" in people. *Love is not a "weakness," "Love" is not gullible. "Love will Hold on"* to what is **"True & Fine."** Willing to give the *benefit of "doubt"* to the individual accused.

Did "Elvis" really abuse His medications? That's a question only "God" knows. For in his illness it's highly "improbable" that He recognized how serious His health condition really was, and how far it had progressed "UNTIL"... it was too late.

Elvis really needed help, but He was a "determined man." As such He was bent on doing it His way, and so He did.

You might recall in his last concert tour in 1977, he sang about facing "The Final Curtain," something He knew was "inevitable," his untimely death. He knew he was sick and He began to understand the issues might be "MORE SERIOUS" than he originally thought. Yes it was now becoming "CLEAR" He would soon face "The Final Curtain."

When Elvis sang "My way"(a song written by Paul Anka, for Frank Sinatra)

He then said, "And now the end is near, and so I face "The Final Curtain," my friends I've made it clear...I've lived a life that's full, I've traveled each and every highway...the record shows I took the blows and did it "My Way."

It's best for us to accept the "Truth," as sad as it may be, and learn from the decisions Elvis made. He was bigger than life and yet is no longer with us in the flesh.

But, the "memories" the "movies" the "music," lingers on, and on and on...

"The Story" about the *"poor boy"* from Tupelo, who was allowed to live a *"fairytale life,"* will be told from generation to generation for as long as this *"Old World"* continues on.

Yes Jesse, *"Elvis"* was able to do for others what *"He"* could not do for himself, *"bring true happiness & "filial"* love and compassion into His life.*"*

He gave these things unselfishly to all but in return received *"disappointment"* from many of His so called *"close friends."*

Yet He would enjoy the uplifting experience, the *"joy"* that He Imparted, through his music, love, and generosity to many who knew him, and to poor souls *"He"* never *"knew,"* yes they all would benefit from this amazing man's *"generosity."*

By the *"Grace of God"* Elvis was able to find the *"Strenght"* to complete His *"77"* Concert Series.

And in just six weeks Elvis would face His *"final Curtain."*

The world is *"Different"* today Jesse, people want to know *"answers,"* why?, how?, is it really true?

Did He really die?

I ask, *"Is it any of our business"* to question *"why?"* Do we really need to know how? And if we are told He has died, should we not be satisfied with *"that"* for an answer, and not try to perpetuate a *"lie"* giving *"false hopes"* to those so very vulnerable, *"The True Fans ... "friends"* of Elvis Aaron Presley?"

Yes, *"friend"* I understand. Thank you for all you have told me.

...... but *"friend"* there is *"one thing"* left I would appreciate hearing.

You said you would relate to me what happened when you went to Elvis' "Memorial Service" and what "you saw" there.

✧

Jesse my "son," Let me begin by saying "Love" although "not gullible" does not rejoice over unrighteousness, but rejoices with "The Truth." It bears all things, "believes" all things, hopes all things, endures all things,

"Love Never Fails."

Elvis taught us that from the Bible also.
(1 Corinthians 13:6-8)

After the meeting that evening which occurred on 8/16/77 I was a "Mess." I went home and cried "uncontrollably." Remember! I was "very young" and a highly emotional young man. At the time it was more than I could bear. I did "NOT" attend the "Memorial," although I was a part of the "Funeral Procession."
The "Memorial Service" conducted by Rex Humbard, at "Graceland" was recorded for me to hear by another one of the "friends." It was 3 months before I could bring myself to listening to the recording. And so I cried again and again.

So I never saw Elvis, but "NONE" of us ever saw Elvis, since the casket He was in was a "Closed One."
When some fans were allowed to view the body, you understand "what they saw."
I'm sure from our conversations you "Understand."
From the "illustration" I used" in explaining it to you, I'm sure you understood "why."

Now you're probably wondering, "How" do we know

"For Sure That He Really Died" since "NONE" of us saw the body?

Jesse Remember THIS! The *"KEY"* to *"understanding"* is *in the "Spelling" of His name on the Memorial Stone at His gravesite.* **"IT" is the proof that "ELVIS" has passed and has been buried there at "Graceland."**

**The "Spelling" of the name "Brings Down"
The
"Final Curtain."**

Elvis "CHANGING" The "Spelling of His Middle Name" *To Honor His <u>Mother's Choice</u> of His "Birth Name" & The "<u>Humility</u>" He Displayed in "Death" <u>to "Yield"</u> to His Father's "Theocratically Assigned" Buriel Position which is next to His Wife Leaving Elvis to be placed not next to His Mother "Whom He Dearly Loved," But next to His Father is an*

<u>*"INCREDIBLE" act of "LOYAL LOVE" on Elvis' Part,*</u>

for His Dear "MOTHER GLADYS"

And He Maintained that "Loyal Love" right up to His "Final Curtain"... His dying day.

Now they all "rest" together at "Graceland" (JOHN 3:16) & (JOHN 5:28& 29)

...the "poor boy" from Tupelo & His family...

THIS is Without a Doubt

"The Love Story Untold"... until now

Do YOU "<u>REALLY</u>" Understand
my "Son," Jesse?"

I then replied to "friend" ... "I DO"

Then It's Time to Stop Breaking "Hearts,"

Jesse "You" Can Make it Happen!

The "Time" Has Come....

My "Son" ....*The "FANS" HAVE "WAITED*
SO LONG"........"YOU ARE THE "ONE"...

"Write the book!"

～◦

The LAST thing "friend" said with "a big smile" on his
face and a "twinkle" in his eyes was ...

T.C.B!

～◦

(Reader please review "friends" explanation of the so
called "misspelling" of the middle name of Elvis.)

～◦

I cried that night and many other nights.
 "friend" was more than a friend to me. He had
  become my "Father." And to my surprise He left me
a note, in an envelope. The "note" Read..."My Dear son
Jesse," may you live a long life and may you always do

what you can to help those who have been carrying
"Heavy Loads" in their lives. Always "Remember Elvis'
words ..." Help your "brother" along the way for the
same God that made YOU made HIM too." God Bless
you, Jesse my "Son,"...see you on the "other side."....
"friend" A.K.A. "William."

I still have Pictures of
Him and I reflect on them often, and if I find
myself starting to "look and search" into things that
are not my business ...

...I quickly recall what he told me long, long,
long ago, on that night ...
"THE NIGHT"
"WE SHARED" our 1st "Candle light Vigil."
"Does not one candle in a room full of darkness make a bright light?"
"Sometimes, Too much light can be Blinding!!

⌒〇

When "friends" Last will & Testament was read, to
my surprise "friend" left me The Restaurant, the
Home I had been living in, and a Very large sum of
money.

All the domestic help was kept
employed by an annuity "friend" set up.

He used me to oversee these funds and the weekly
distribution to all the domestic help.

This to me was a "fairytale" experience.

Then I thought of Elvis when He sang "fairytale."

I understood "now" more than ever what He meant.
He had lived a "fairytale existence." And Now "I" was
being allowed to be part of that "fairytale." Another
"Dream come True."

# # #

Yes, This "Fairytale would be "passed on from one generation to another"... a never ending Love story! One day "I" would find the "One" who would take my place, and "He" would become "friend." The "Fairytale" "Lives On" as another is privileged to be part of the

"Never Ending Love Story"
The Final Curtain a Love Story Untold? ...
No!... but to be Told Again and Again and Again...!

What a "gift" The *"poor boy"* **from Tupelo has left us!**
"Yes my friends
Elvis, Even in "Death,"
continues...To
"Make Dreams Come True!"
May all Your Dreams also Come True and may you too find the "Truth" found in God's Word as Elvis Certainly did! *(Psalm83:18)*
God Bless ... "friendfromyesteryear"

"TO THE PRESLEY FAMILY"

What Shall "We" Say?
Perhaps... "Thank you,"
"Miss Lisa Marie"& "Miss Priscilla"
For Sharing "Your Father" with us and & for all The hard work you & your Mother have done in keeping "Graceland" so Beautifull!
Only a "Loving Mother & Daughter" could do such a thing, and so we thank you. "Thanks" also for...

"Opening the door" to your Home,

Inviting us in as "guests" into "Graceland."
The "Memories" your father,

"Elvis Aaron Presley"

have shared so generously with us
will remain deep within our "Hearts"
"May" the "Fairytale Continue to be Told" for "Your
father" has taught us much
about "love, life, and "sharing."
May God Bless You
"Miss Lisa Marie, & "Miss Priscilla" & your family"

Signed ... Your "Daddy's" fans from all over the
World !
&
"friendfromyesteryear"

∽♥

"Reflections..."
Yes on that "Fateful" day so, so, long ago,
a "silence" fell over those gathered in Memphis.
But an even Larger "Silence" fell over the entire
world as millions mourned the "passing" of their friend,
"Elvis Aaron Presley"...
A "Silence" that would "Unite" peoples of all races
and creeds, at least for a short period of time
in this world "Divided by "Race." "False Religion,"
and One's "National Origin" etc. etc. etc.

A "TIDAL" Wave would begin to rise and surge.
Its "Echo" would reverberate throughout all
"History"...The "Fairytale" Elvis sang about in His Final
"77" Tour had come to an end.

But was it Really "The" End?

No my friends, as in every "Fairytale" a "Moral" is entertained. This "Fairytale" like any other, would be told again and again. One generation to another, time and again.

The Moral of his story is simple, although "Breathtaking"... Elvis Aaron Presley came from absolute "poverty" to become probably "The Greatest Entertainer" the world has ever known. He never forgot his "roots" and never did He think of himself as someone "special."

"Graceland," the Home of "Elvis Aaron Presley" will stand NOT as a Home of a man of "Great Wealth" but rather as a
"Monument"
of a "poor boy's
Love
for his **Momma."**

Yes it was for Gladys, his mother, that He purchased "Graceland for 100 thousand dollars." (By today's standards probably equal to 10 million dollars.)

What a gift The "poor boy" from Tupelo has left us!

So let us now "pause" for a moment, close your eyes and visualize...

Friends, have you ever "wished" for something special?

Have you ever "dreamed" of something special?

"Elvis made "Dreams" come true."

Many have never given thought to the millions of Jobs Created by Elvis....Untold numbers of "Elvis

Tribute Singers" who have the opportunity to make a good living imitating the "poor boy from Tupelo." Staggering "numbers" of merchants who sell CD's, DVD's, memorabilia, etc. of Elvis.

To this day, Elvis Presley's Organization continues to support, very generously, many charities, a "Legacy that will continue on probably until "This world is Gone."

Not bad for The "poor boy from Tupelo", who started life with nothing!

So tell me friends, What do YOU have to say about this "gift" that WE were given?

I say...... He made us smile, laugh,

dance and at times even shed a tear. Yes Elvis gave it all !

Right to the "END"......

When asked by a dear friend of Elvis why Elvis was now surprising him with the keys to a brand new Cadillac, Elvis simply said, "What good is *fame and fortune if* you have no one to *share it with?"*

Yes, "Elvis" made "Dreams come True!"

So did "Elvis Aaron Presley" really die on August 16, 1977?

Well, when you ask about "dying" what do you consider as "Dead?"

I see Elvis Presley as a man who lives on in the "Hearts" and "Minds" of millions. That being the case His "Story" will be told from one generation to another.

"May the Fairytale Continue to be Told".....For it has taught us much about "love, life, and "sharing."

A "Fairytale?" you ask?

Maybe..... But of a "Real Man" And you know "friends"... "Fairytales" have happy endings and this one will also.

The Final Chapter of "This Book" is yet to be completed...We "Respectfully" leave that for you Miss Lisa Marie, if and when you should choose to do so. There are many stories that may yet be told but only "You," with all your "memories" & "friends" could accomplish such a task.

Maybe "Graceland" or E.P.E. could "Reconsider" releasing The "77" "Final Concert Tour" on Blue Ray DVD.

We loved Elvis right to the end. His appearance and performances perhaps were not up to the standard the family believes would qualify for release. We understand their feelings and respect them for wanting to preserve Elvis' Honor. But as his fans we would hope "they" would give serious thought to reconsidering their decision. We would truly be grateful for the release of that concert series including the CBS Special both "Edited" and "Unedited." We loved Him to the end, regardless of looks, as far as we are concerned he looked Great! But we will respect "YOUR" decision.

January 16, 2015 would be a Great Time to release such a...

"Royal Gift."

"So in conclusion... I hope my fictional story has sent the proper "Message" to all concerned, and I certainly hope it has shown proper "Respect" for the "Presley Family," especially Elvis' "little sweetheart, Lisa Marie"...& her mother

"Miss Priscilla"

Thank You... "Miss Lisa Marie, & "Miss Priscilla"

Signed ..."Your friends from all over the World" &.......

friendfromyesteryear...God Bless!

Chapter 22

"The End"?

⤮

T his is your chapter "Miss Lisa Marie" should you chose to complete it....Thank you .... "friendfromyesteryear"

⤮

To My "friends"...
"ELVIS AARON PRESLEY " was not a "Perfect" man, nor was He a "fictional" Character. He was neither a "God" to be worshiped, nor a "saint" to be adored, but Elvis WAS a "Real Man," who "Cared & Loved Much."... God indeed "Blessed" The "poor boy" from Tupelo...
It has been said a persons success in "Life" is not measured by how much one loves,
but rather by how much one is "loved by others," and
"Elvis Aaron Presley" was loved
"by millions!"

He has taught us much about "love, life, and "sharing."

Yes, *"the poor boy from Tupelo,"* showed us true Riches..... *"A Good "Relationship With One's Creator,"* loyalty, respect, generosity, and most of all *"LOVE."*

And so He rests peacefully. We await our seeing Him again as Elvis knew and believed what is stated at *John3:16 & 5:28 & 29* ...The words of his Lord and savior Jesus Christ, when *"Jesus said:*

"Do not marvel, because there is going to be a resurrection of the Dead!" And The Earth will be restored to it's original paradise condition as it was in the beginning. Those *"sleeping"* in *"Death"* will awaken to live forever on a restored *"Paradise Earth!* Our Dear *"friend"* Elvis, will walk this earth again, along with His Mother, Father, family and millions of *"friends"*(Psalm 37: 29) If you would like to know more about this *"Hope"* feel free to speak with me..."friendfromyesteryear" I would consider it a privelage to proclaim Elvis' Hope for it **was** this, Elvis would proclaim to whomever would listen.

<u>I personally look forward to that day,</u> so very close at hand. How about you, all you millions of fans and supporters? Elvis would undoubtedly say *"Look"* into God's Word and see for yourself....... It's a *"Beautiful Hope"* "guaranteed" by Jesus Christ himself!

<u>And so to "YOU," my "friends", from all</u> around the world, may the *"God of all tender mercies, who gives peace, grant you comfort in all your "Tribulations,"* and may you have *"Peace"* in your *"Lives."*.

It has been the aim of this book to bring *"Peace"* & a *"Smile"* of approval on the faces of all who have loved

Elvis Aaron Presley, as an entertainer, philanthropist, humanitarian, family member and "friend."

Hopefully I have accomplished that goal. The proof will be in "your hands" as to how this book is received by the public, and of course "Miss Lisa Marie," "Miss Priscilla," & All "Presley" family members.

This has been a "Fictional" account of the events leading up to 8/16/1977 the "Passing of our friend "Elvis Aaron Presley" and subsequent "fictional events" leading down to modern times.

Hopefully I haven't stepped on anyone's "Toes," If so, I apologize, it certainly was not my intention know-ingly, or unknowingly. This book has been a "look" at a story better than 35 years old "told" from a "differing" *viewpoint.* So as I've often said, "Opinions are like noses, everyone has one"....this has been mine.............. and so...

When one comes to the end of a story it then becomes time to
"Close the Book."
Thank you my "friends" "from around the world."
"I sincerely hope"
<u>"The Final Curtain a Love Story Untold"</u>
(until now) Has given you all some "food for thought" a little "laughter,"

a "smile" and "Peace in your Hearts."
May "God Bless you all"…
Signed by…… *"an old man with a very*
happy & "interesting life"…… *"friendfromyesteryear"& of course*
my "friend" & "little consultant"… **"Mystrykitty"**..
Signed… "friendfromyesteryear"

CPSIA information can be obtained at www.ICGtesting.com
Printed in the USA
LVOW07s0042300715

448123LV00021B/251/P

9 781500 696511